THE LAST CITY

After The AI Apocalypse

Madhu Chittarvu

ISBN 979-8-89475-351-5

All the characters and places in this book are fictitious and created for a futuristic science fiction creative story. Any resemblance to any place or individual or incidents is not intentional but fictitious and coincidental.

Contents

Contents

Foreword

During the last few years a revolutionary development has taken place in our lives. It is the advent of Artificial intelligence in every field of human activity. The availability of ChatGpt and other innovations like large language models and Generative AI in learning and creating data and information has been extraordinary. Machine learning, deep learning, and neural networks have grown enormously in Medicine, Computers Economics Defence even Agriculture and almost all such fields of Science. I am a doctor by profession practising Medicine Cardiology and Diabetology, but a writer by aptitude. I have been interested in writing Science Fiction and have been a recognised Sci-Fi writer in the South Indian language of Telugu. I have written the Space Opera trilogy of "War for Mars a story of the fourth millennium" and published in this Kindle self publishing platform of Amazon almost ten years ago. They are available as e books and paper backs even now.

Apart from this I have written nearly 6 Sci-fi novels in the Telugu language and about 60 stories also in Telugu and published 3 story anthologies in Telugu two of them mainly Sci-fi.

I was fascinated by the topic of possibilities of AI dominating human life and systems as machines acquire autonomy and their own intelligence. This novel "The Last City" is written with this dystopian concept and the human resilience in rebuilding the destroyed civilization. I hope this will be an interesting and thought provoking read for those who are interested in reading Science Fiction.

I have taken inputs about the aftermath of nuclear war and the possible scenario from the AI sources of Microsoft Bing and Copilot and modified according to my story with Indian background. I created the cover with Wonder app and was permitted to use it by these apps. I acknowledge their help.

It was thrilling for me to create such a dystopian yet possible Science Fiction novel with modern gadgets of AI itself. This could be the first novel in India acknowledging the helpful inputs of AI for some information though the concept is my own.

This proves my point of AI becoming more powerful in future and the scientists must employ suitable safeguards to prevent the machines making errors or dominating us. The flip side is that AI has tremendous utility in guiding our lives better too in all fields like Diagnostic Medicine, Information technology and other human Sciences.

On this hopeful note I end my introduction and welcome you to read the novel.

Madhu Chittarvu MD

Chapter 1

Forest

No one knew or predicted it before.

Not in the wildest imaginations of a Doomsday writer or fantasy films.

Not by journalists, not by wild YouTube gossipers, not even by the experts sitting in the think tanks of the ministry of Defence.

There was no suspicion of even a little tension political or economic, no expansionist dictator aspiring to expand his territorial ambitions or economic greed.

Delhi was calm Mumbai was tranquil, Chennai was singing its eternal peaceful devotional songs, Hyderabad was having its night life with *qawwalis* and *kebabs* while deep south at the tip of India, Kerala had revelled in its quiet backwaters and *kathakali* and Kanyakumari slept amidst the roar of the three seas after watching a glorious amber sunset that evening to the roaring delight of multitudes of tourists.

It was past mid night and Asha did not expect it too. She was fast asleep in the wooden house shaped like a tent in the thick of the jungle away from the hustle and bustle of the city and her arm was around her boyfriend's neck, who was fast asleep in a deep dreamless slumber. They were almost naked, exhausted from a night of passionate lovemaking and ecstasy of champagne and the wild delicious meat snacks offered by the forest guest house management.

The sound like the distant thunder did not awaken them first. Then it gradually grew into a rumble and then a loud but distant bang.

It was the cries of the birds and the wailing of wolves and roaring of hidden tigers that awakened them. When Asha opened her eyes the first thing she noticed was the faint smell of burning from afar. It was musty, smelling like burning coal tar and the nauseating feeling of human flesh in flames somewhere.

Then the distant rumbles. They were 100 kilometres away from Delhi in a deep jungle and in an isolated guest house and the holiday home was very special for it had the luxuries befitting those of VIPs only. And for the last two days Asha and Sathya were living there after a heavy work in their respective fields on a well-deserved holiday.

There was internet with state-of-the-art communication systems, a security fencing fitted with electric wire and a few officers of the security forces two kilometres away watching over their safety.

For her father would not agree her to be alone and left unguarded even if it was only a holiday with her boyfriend whom she thinks he does not know but he is fully aware of.

"Do not loiter in the jungle in the night. Reach your home early. And keep in touch with security guards for anything you need."

He told her hugging her for the last time before she left in a land cruiser for her foray into the forest.

"I do not ask who he is. But be careful with your boyfriend. Do not reveal any state secrets to him whatever the circumstances. Enjoy well but take care."

He gave her a small black box with a golden symbol of Om on it and with a code lock and spoke. "Keep this with you. Remember the code word only in your mind." He whispered in her ear. It is Rakshana2044. Your mother's name. It contains the help you need in an emergency. Once you open it you should be able to understand how to use it. OK?

I need not tell you more. You are the deputy minister of technology in my cabinet."

He was a good father and a doting father and a clever father. He never interfered with her private life. He was a democrat hundred per cent and respected human rights and the welfare of the poor at any cost. He was admired, worshipped and venerated all over India. He was her father Vikram Rao the Prime Minister of India who was just elected unanimously by his party for he won 400 of the 650 parliament seats and came to power in Delhi only a year ago.

And she was Asha Rao the only daughter of the PM.

But even she did not know how and why the end came.

The burning smell, the smoke at a distance and the flickering light of flames said it all. India was in a conflagration and the distant Delhi, and all other cities were burning. And burning in a moment with a bang in the mid night.

The just awakened Sathya shouted, "Asha what is it?" "I think it is the end." Asha said, "The apocalypse. Everything is burning with a bang. It is the war. The last war which ends all wars, and this war came without a warning."

"But how and why?"

It is only possible by a series of nuclear attacks. And we are being attacked…and everything is already destroyed. It cannot happen so swiftly otherwise." "We are lucky that we are in a forest. Let's go out and see!" Sathya said.

Both ran out of the cottage and looked outside. It was dark with lots of sounds of animals and birds screeching in the forest. "Go and watch the computer! And call your security!" shouted Sathya. "After all you have a private security communication with your bodyguards and your father."

Asha went back into the front room of the cottage and quickly put on the computer on the table. There was some power still in the cottage for the nuclear attack has not spread into the forest yet and it operated by a generator powered by solar energy in the day and nuclear power in the night. She took the mobile phone and called the security number 999.

"Hello! Hello! Anybody is there?"

Silence.

No one was talking. Asha tried the news search on the YouTube app which was still existing in 2041 too.

The screen went blank but then a message blinking from the news channel in red letters scrolled across the screen.

"This is the New Delhi TV reporting. The capital city Delhi has been attacked and destroyed all offices of the Government. Everything is in ruins and flames.

A nuclear war has started not only here but possibly all over the world. It is the end of the capital and ruling Government. No one knows about the fate of Army, Air force headquarters and the defence systems. It is chaos all around.

I am now hiding in a bunker. And I cannot tell anything more. More people like me have found this and we are crammed in a congested place to escape the radiation. Putting this on my mobile hoping this may reach all." Sonu Mehta reporting.

Asha put her head in both her hands in shock and cried. "Oh Daddy! What happened to you? Where are you?"

"Go to CNN, BBC, Asian news and search for the latest news" Sathya shouted in a voice full of animated anxiety.

"I am doing just that."

Asha was browsing through all the channels and flipped on the smart stream news which was coming and then was lost in a minute. The computer had a glass screen where the text or images appear like a hologram in front of your face and eyes. But it was blank everywhere.

"Let us wait. I can't believe this. Okay, it is as if strikes and counter strikes, first attacks and second attacks have happened spontaneously without the control of anyone and the information system Internet system and the 10G communication system, everything is lost.

And lost in a jiffy. So strong is the impact of the nuclear attack. But surely, I can tell only after an hour or two. I wish it could be a glitch or false alarm but with the state of the equipment I have, I am sure the system has failed definitely and completely. It is destroyed all over the world."

"But why? Sathya asked. "There was never any indication of any bad intentions either in our enemy countries like Pakistan or China, or a war in Europe or US. Why should the world be destroyed at all? I earnestly hope that it is your wildest imagination."

I hope it could be only any imagination, but you must realise that I am the deputy minister of technology in the government, and I do know such a thing is always possible. But only once in one million times.

"But how?"

"Our defence systems are all automated now for the last decade or so. The AI automatically activates the nuclear missiles if it suspects an attack. They can fire even without human verification to save time. I noticed this risk and many times argued in the conferences to regulate this anomaly in our nuclear missile retaliatory system. The Generals and defence committee members always vetoed me. This was because our adversaries were having the same systems, and we cannot afford to change to old systems. But any unknown error in the coding system of AI can cause the system to fire in an emergency."

"But how can you think it is a war between India and its enemies? It could be anywhere in the world which started attacks and counter attacks between countries and started a chain reaction."

"You are right. It could have started in China or USA or Russia or any other smaller nuclear states. We might have been involved in a chain reaction."

"But the result is the same. It is the destruction of every country. The Earth itself?'

"Do not come to any quick conclusions! Let us explore the forest and find my security van and its staff. Go in and pack up your things. A torch and a gun and gum boots and night glasses."

"But the radiation… and think of the animals prowling around and the next attack may come any time soon."

"No worry. We are many kilometres away. The radiation will come here in a few days only, not now. The bombing would be on nuclear installations army and Headquarters cities like Delhi or Agra and the like. They don't bomb remote jungles like this. But the real problem may start in a few weeks depending on the extent of damage and radiation. Let us go and see."

"OK. As you say Minister!" Sathya smiled benignly. "We will soon find out."

There were more sounds of wolves howling, roaring tigers and lions and birds fluttering their wings. Then there was silence only interrupted by the screeching sound of crickets.

Sathya went in. Asha also went in and searched for all the necessary equipment for the long trek in the forest.

They needed food, water, protective equipment like helmets and bullet proof vests and arms like guns to protect themselves from animals which were obviously in terror. They got ready in an hour. It was 2:00 AM in the night and they stepped out setting to the dark jungle with howling noises off and on and thousands of blinking lights of firefly insects in the bushes. They had a Land Rover in front of the cottage. Asha said, "Let's try the Land Rover. It may be safe for us to drive than trek as it has a mounted focusing light and again all the communication equipment needed, with food supplies. It is also bulletproof."

"Of course, yes. We cannot walk in such a situation even though it's only a bare two kilometres from the security van."

The land rover just started moving on the bumpy road of the jungle with shadows of trees on either side and only the headlights illuminating the path in front of them in a circular serpentine grassy path. Soon they were at the lodge where the security van was situated, and the staff lived temporarily to guard them.

There was smoke and fire emanating from the lodge. The security van was empty but it's lights were blinking. Asha and Sathya got down from the Land Rover and ran into the lodge. Wooden doors, cement walls and floors made an eerie sound as they searched the rooms. Asha tried all the electric switches, but the lights were not coming on.

"It's a power failure. I don't know why. There should be a generator here somewhere. Then she gasped as she focused the torchlight on the bodies motionless on the floor. Four uniformed soldiers were lying motionless on the floor with blood oozing from their chest wounds. Obviously, they were fired upon from a close range by guns and were killed in cold blood.

"This means the killers came for me and there could be a hunt for us. A coup in Delhi and some assassins came for us to exterminate us. It may not be the nuclear attack" cried Asha in a terrifying realisation. "Run! Sathya run into the jungle and let us hide. They have gone to the cottage searching for us and now they will be back any time soon here. They will see the land rover parked here. Let us slip into the back of this place and walk into the bushes."

As she said this, there was machine gun staccato fire and the sound of explosion from outside pierced their ear drums.

Looking out, Sathya gasped. "The Land rover is burning. They are already here."

There was no time to think. Both ran through the back door into the darkness. They ran without looking back into the bushes and plant groves and even as she thought of the conspiracy and annihilation of her father's Government, Asha remembered her dad giving her the device and telling the security password. Did he have a premonition of this? Did he expect her to survive and save the country? Could she?

"At any cost do not give the device or share the password. It will save you."

Sathya was her loving boyfriend and a qualified pilot of planes and even had training as an astronaut. He was close to her. But she could not reveal anything to him too. After all there is something bigger going on. She had luckily her handbag fitted with a metal chain to her hand. It contained the mobile phone with smart stream and a few other gadgets and the device too. She never forgot to carry this.

But all other necessary equipment communications video phones arms...everything was in the Land rover.

After running breathlessly for half hour in the bushy rock ridden jungle, they stopped for breath and looked back. Soon it would be dawn.

The security cottage and their land rover were burning in flames at a distance. The flame illuminated the surroundings in flickering shadows, but the saboteurs or assassins were not visible.

Did they see them? Would they find them? It was a worrying question. They would not leave them, and It was not possible as they did not have any clue where they were. The mobile in her bag was switched off and would not give her position as the communications system and

Global positioning system were destroyed apparently in the nuclear war as she found out just a while ago.

"Let's go! And hide. It is a coup, and someone pulled the plug on my dad and a coup just happened. There seems to be an error and the nuclear war has started and destroyed the world. But these people want to get rid of me as I am the PM's daughter."

"The plot thickens."Sathya smiled a derisive smile, "…and I am caught with you in the political coup. Unexpectedly. I like mysteries. But of course, I am with you. Loyal!"

"Yeah, before a tiger or lion eats us. Or radiation causes damage in a few days. But we have to find out who is behind all this. And we have to go to the bottom of this whole episode. We must survive first".

It was nearing five hours after midnight. Soon there would be dawn.

They walked searching for shelter and a hiding place before the Sunrise.

At a far distance surrounding the burning cottage four human shapes were walking in radiation suits and helmets which blocked their speech and allowed them to communicate only by walkie- talkies to each other.

"This doesn't look good. They must have escaped into the jungle. We searched for five hours. One man of ours was moulded by a tiger, and another of our colleagues was bitten by a mad wolf needing medical treatment. I have talked to the General. He said that there is no issue, we can always go back into the jungle in the next few days."

They walked and went to a hiding place in a clearing where the vehicle was hidden. It was an armoured truck with antennae fixed on the top and search lights illuminating the forest in front but now no longer needed as the sunlight was shining in orange colour on the green grass leading to the highway.

The day after, it dawned in the forest and the vehicle moved with a dead man and the groaning man bitten by the outraged wolf.

It was the apocalypse, and the earth was ending all over the world, only they did not know it. Neither their boss who had ordered the coup in the capital, without knowing the consequences.

But now there was no safety for anyone either in the capital or in the surroundings.

As usual soldiers were only the victims, and their rulers always escaped and hid in safety.

Chapter 2

Apocalypse

Samar Singh was tense as he watched the TV monitors in front of him. In front of him the TV unfolded horrible scenes. Someone had taken the photo of the big mushroom cloud above the capital city. Buildings there were in flames everywhere, dark smoke engulfed the city of Delhi with all the highways blocked with debris of buildings and burning cars and vehicles. Pictures showed airport burning and train stations severely damaged and collapsing. One picture showed people running with their children on their shoulders and suddenly falling on the ground.

Samar Singh never expected this in his wildest of dreams. The idea was surely a revolution and displacement of the PM Vikram Rao and his inefficient government by all means. There were arguments with him before he had planned all this with meticulous details. He would sit in PM Rao's office and ask him for reforms like centralization of the economy, increase of taxes, increase of payment for the military and a religious unitary dictatorship. Vikram Rao was his friend for a long time. He was a fool in Samar

Singh's view no doubt, pursuing welfare economics and wasting most of the national resources for giving funds to the poor people who brought nothing back. There was more to do, many more business houses to promote many more industries to and expand the national boundaries. This was the only way for India to become a superpower. Not only in Asia but in the world. This was the only way to beat another gigantic power in Asia that is China and the world powers like the USA with its allies. The country needed to have a restructure with strong discipline and hard work to improve the exports and GDP especially as a nuclear power and military power. India needed to occupy the surrounding countries which are too small to fight. They can be integrated at utilised to improve the economy to help India to become a superpower. This was Samar Singh's view. Such arguments raged between them frequently. Once Vikram Rao was elected PM and he himself was promoted as General, he always met him at the weekends in private capacity to put forth his proposals.

"Vikram! Democracy is not good for this country. Make the people work! Do not give them sops and freebies. It is a waste to have equality to the states or the corrupt politicians who are the chief ministers in those various capitals. Let us declare an emergency. Buy more arms, buy more weapons, buy more modern systems. We will attack whoever attacks us, but defence is not enough. We must occupy the buffer states at the borders, which are too small to improve their economies and will become a gigantic subcontinent and will have great influence at least in Southeast Asia."

"You are mistaken Samar. This country cannot be ruled by a dictatorship. The people are seemingly mild, but they are very tough. I'm a democrat and respect all people of all economic groups and religions. I believe in welfare economics. As it is, we have the latest artificial intelligence systems which can attack anybody who attacks us. We have nuclear bombs, even a few hydrogen bombs on missile systems which can go up to 4000 kilometres, having in range the capitals of China, Pakistan, Sri Lanka and all such countries. We cannot use them for offence and we use them only for our defence and security. Our economy is good and is growing. And we will utilise the money for the welfare of the poorest of the poor. Still, we are one of the most populous countries in this world in fact the most populated with the highest population surpassing even China now. But we have got lot of work force and educated people now though poverty is still consuming us. I believe in democratic growth and equality and helping the poor people with incentives to develop themselves. We cannot certainly improve the defence budget at the expense of the budget for the poor. Of course, we have been friends from school days, and we happen to be in the top positions now. Of course, your views are yours, my views are mine. But I am the elected and committed leader of the people. Mine will prevail."

Thus, the arguments went on and on. And Samar Singh decided this had to change. He had access to all defence establishments strategic reports equipment and artificial intelligence systems. Slowly he developed a coterie of his own with similar views. They had meetings secretly every month in Shimla, Dehradun and in Chennai, even in Mumbai. The plan was hatched and would have been executed meticulously with a bloodless revolution removing Vikram Rao and establishing a military government.

It did not happen. It had to happen two nights ago with army tanks and the revolutionary pilots of the Air Force guarding the Airways and Samar Singh himself going to the PM's office and telling him to resign peacefully and go to prison. The parliament would be sealed, the ministries would be occupied with soldiers and rule of martial law would have been declared in the country through all media. His views would have been explained to all the population through all the TV channels. All the Naval Military and Air Force command centres in the country would have come under his sole command. A new India would have started. By the time it all started at midnight Samar Singh took off in his military jeep with a convoy of tanks and was travelling on the road leading to the PM's house, the Presidential building and to the ministerial blocks.

Then it all happened suddenly.

The siren was sounding like the wailing of a wolf or an owl at the same time. All the TVs went blank and then all the mobiles went blank. Then the TVs announced a warning that a nuclear attack was in the offing and all the citizens were advised to go to the nearest nuclear shelters or leave the city in their vehicles within 15 minutes. There was only one nuclear bunker in the centre of the capital and one nuclear shelter on the road to Agra. "This is a warning given by the automatic defence system and it is not a drill. The missiles are coming from China in the North and Pakistan in the West. It is advised that all citizens should vacate the capital and travel as much distance as possible from the city because the likelihood of security is more far from the City of Delhi. Warnings like this flashed again and again on the mobile screens too. And now General Samar Singh who planned his revolt and takeover of the government found himself in the military bunker along with his driver and security guards and just a few officers of his most confidential coterie. They were some of the top military Air Force and naval officials. He had the presence of mind to use his own private secret security phone system. And most of them could reach the nuclear bunker which was his top-secret place by the side of the Delhi Agra highway. Many could manage to bring their families also along. Some civilian ministers whom he recruited into the revolution like the finance minister the defence minister, the home minister, the Home Secretary and their families could reach this place.

And then the apocalypse came. It was the explosion of explosions which destroyed everything.

"Thanks, General Samar, for saving us. But how did it all happen without your knowledge? The whole country is attacked by nuclear bombs, and it is the disaster and apocalypse of the whole world and in India. But how?"

"The unexpected always happens. Something happened in the artificial intelligence-controlled defence system. Or someone must have leaked about our plans to the PM who is the person who has access to the defence warning system which is final and ultimate. He must have pulled some buttons in his anxiety or fear. I have done some mistakes and caused all this catastrophe. He was always a fool making mistakes always. But do not worry. I have contingency plans for just such a situation. There is always a possibility of a war which happened in ten other countries and has involved us. Whatever it is the radiation is going to be there the damage is going to be there for at least a month. We will see what we can do for helping the injured and the damaged cities. We will construct them again. I am now ordering for all the emergency radiation protocol and the measures to be taken. We will operate from a bunker and recruit all the doctors, radiation experts and rescue teams. But we are at a disadvantage as all the communication systems, transport systems and the infrastructure have completely failed. It is the proverbial end of the days. Vikram Rao the PM who must have died already is totally responsible for this. Let us not lose heart and determine to rebuild the country and the cities again. I am now asking all the radiation experts in the army who are here and in other places to prepare a report and a plan for rehabilitation and the measures to be taken for treating the nuclear damage to people and property. Even if it was an enemy who has done this, we will retaliate."

It was a great speech. The top officials of the military and civilian ministries assembled there clapped in appreciation and murmured "General, we are with you!"

What happened next was hectic but methodical and planned but it had taken six months time for them to rebuild and rehabilitate a completely damaged capital city. But the rest of the country was totally damaged and anarchic.

It was the dawn of the age of post-apocalyptic India.

It was a dark anarchic cold prolonged nuclear winter. With acid rains shortage of food and water, completely damaged transport systems of trains and planes and communications, the first week after the explosion was horrible.

The blast was so powerful that it shattered windows and toppled buildings for miles around. A mushroom cloud rose over the city, spreading radioactive dust and smoke. The air was filled with screams and sirens, but soon they were silenced by the shockwave and the firestorm.

The survivors who were not killed instantly by the blast or the radiation suffered from severe burns, nausea, vomiting, hair loss, and bleeding. Many of them died within hours or days, unable to find medical help or clean water. Some of them tried to flee the city, but were met with chaos and violence on the roads. Looters, gangs, and militias fought for the scarce resources and territory. Some of the refugees were captured and enslaved by ruthless hooligans looking for food and money.

The city became a wasteland, a hell on earth. The sky was darkened by the nuclear winter, blocking out the sun and lowering the temperature. The crops failed and the animals died. The water was contaminated, and the soil was poisoned. The radiation caused mutations and diseases in the plants and wildlife. The few people who remained in the city struggled to survive, scavenging for food and shelter, hiding from the raiders and the mutants. The first week after the nuclear attack was the beginning of the end for Delhi and its surroundings. It was the start of a new era of darkness and despair for humanity.

But then Samar Singh the General and his team slowly came out of the bunkers after a week. They were cautious and were handicapped by the lack of radiation suits for protection. But then they came in teams and surveyed the scene. The city and surroundings were already in the hands of warlords and some militia and there were riots for food and water too. No one knew what happened after but India and Pakistan both thought that the other has attacked it. India had also thought that China attacked it. No one knew what happened till a long time.

Least of all Asha and Sathya who were in a forest guest house and had no clue of what happened. Asha only thought of her father's warning and the device.

And they started walking in the forest with only a bag of clothes and a mobile which was dead and a few gadgets like torches rope and a pocket knife.

Asha knew she had the device but did not talk about it to Sathya.

Meanwhile the General who planned to imprison Asha and the PM was himself trapped in the bunker.

No one knew what was happening except the other states of India which escaped the severity of the bombing. With damage of various severities, the union broke, and the world was aghast but did not venture to help for a long time and the neighbouring countries closed their borders for refugees.

The warlords were former military officers, politicians, businessmen, or criminals who had access to weapons, vehicles, and followers. They used their power and influence to seize control of the areas around the city, exploiting the people and the resources. They fought each other for dominance, forming alliances and betrayals. Some of them claimed to have a vision for the future, a new order or a new religion. Others were driven by greed, ambition, or madness. They were the new rulers of the post-apocalyptic world.

The rest of India was also affected by the nuclear attack on Delhi, but in different ways. According to some sources India and Pakistan came close to a nuclear war after the attack, as both sides accused each other of violating the No First Use doctrine2 that they had pledged to follow. The international community intervened to prevent a full-scale nuclear escalation, but the tensions remained high, and the relations deteriorated.

Other parts of India also faced the consequences of the nuclear fallout, such as radiation exposure, environmental damage, food insecurity, and health problems. Some regions were more vulnerable than others, depending on their proximity to the blast site, their level of development, and their access to resources. Some states tried to cope with the crisis by providing aid and shelter to the refugees, while others tried to exploit the situation by asserting their autonomy or seceding from the union. The central government struggled to maintain its authority and legitimacy, as it faced internal and external challenges.

The nuclear attack on Delhi also had an impact on India's relations with other countries, especially China. China was seen as a potential threat by India, as it had a larger and more advanced nuclear arsenal and had border disputes with India. China also had strategic interests in Pakistan, as part of its Belt and Road Initiative. China tried to balance its role as a mediator and a competitor in the region, while also pursuing its own interests and agenda. The nuclear attack on Delhi changed the balance of power and security in South Asia and created new opportunities and risks for all the actors involved.

Of course, all this was not known to Asha and Sathya.

"There must be surely other cities which survived the attack. Let us walk! "Asha said. But in her mind, she had the electronic device looking like a circular disc which was given by her dad.

"As if I have another option!' Sathya tried to make light of the situation.

After two hours of walking, they were lucky to reach a spot where there were trees giving shade from the Sun and a small stream with clear water flowing with the rays of sun shining on it like silver streaks

Let us camp here. Asha said. Please stay here I want to go behind the bushes to...

"I know. Go ahead, "said Sathya.

As she finished her calls of nature and washed the first thing Asha did was to take out the device. Was it a pen drive? Did it need a laptop or computer to read the contents? But she had none.

She examined and tried pressing the various small dot like codes on it.

It went on for fifteen minutes,

Are you Ok? Sathya called.

"Coming" she said. She had to give up accessing the device?

Then something happened. Some button or a code suddenly activated and a flash of hologram with the image of her father Vikram Rao the PM shone before her. He was talking many things but the most important was only one sentence…

Asha was astonished and started to hear the message. There was a lot her dad talked and then the most important was…

"…If you have a paper, note down the coordinates for bunker or just hear and memorize. The hologram of Rao was talking. This is all about saving yourselves from the radiation and the nuclear fallout after a possible sabotage on me…"

She did not have a paper. The only option was to memorise. 80 2E and 30.5N .

"It must be a forest near you. I'm assuming that you are somewhere near the Rishikesh forest guest house. You see, you have a compass in your phone. You can search for the latitude and longitude. And below a big Banyan tree which is conspicuous. You can find a big circular metal disc on the ground underneath the leaves. If you clear the leaves, you will find a door. With a coding on the top and a slot for the password which I have told you "*Rakshana*

2044." It will open. And there will be a staircase leading down to a large bunker. Your hand is the passkey to open the door. In fact, all the bunkers have your handprint as the passkey to enter in the country. Remember there is also a slot for retinal check if something goes wrong. There in the bunker you can find food, clothes, some communication equipment, radiation-protection suits, water and there is also an oxygen plant. There is electricity produced by a generator. These will last for 6 months for you. Once the radiation threat is gone, you can come out. You may find some gadgets there. Like computers. And yeah, a humanoid robot which is programmed to help you and your friend to further travel and take decisions. Take care. This I am telling you because I'm not sure whether I will live or not. will try my best to survive the sabotage by General Samar. My dear *beti* it will be tough. You will have to continue my legacy as a democrat and protector of the people from the possible future dictator who is going to harass the people. God bless you". The communication ended.

A wave of fear and then sadness engulfed her. What was happening? She could never imagine that in her wildest dreams that her dad would be attacked in a coup by the seemingly friendly "uncle" Samar Singh. But then why this nuclear attack? One possibility was that dad would have done some mistake in his anxiety to save the country from a dictator? As far as she can decipher a military revolt cannot plan a self-destructive nuclear attack. Something happened somewhere in the defence system. But now she must escape to the bunker.

"Come on Sathya! It is the survival now which is paramount for soon radiation may come here though we are away. I happen to know a place. Walk now still when we have light!"

They both started walking in the dense jungle. It was gloomy and uncertain way but a *koel* still cooed from somewhere in the trees. And the golden rays of the Sun occasionally fell on them while they started trekking.

Chapter 3

Coup

Vikram Rao was sitting in his chair in a remote underground bunker under the ground of Hyderabad Deccan and was talking to his closest adviser Niranjan Phalke about the catastrophe that happened. In fact, the PM was on the run away from Delhi days before the coup attempt on him. He reached Hyderabad *incognito*. There was little else he could do as it was obvious according to his secretary and close aides that all his cabinet has been bought by some adversary. They are all for installing Samar Singh as the new ruler. The military will march, and the Air Force will guard them from above and the foreign powers are supporting them. "Not in the least, it is the new rulers of China who want you out and install the Military here as they promised to protect their belt and road project and flourishing business in this area and with the western world. It saved them a long sea route through the China sea and Indian Ocean." He was warned. He tried to contact the Secretary of State in USA and the British PM and the Australian PM who were the partners of a defence treaty against China from a long time. They said there is no intelligence of such sort.

They suggested reforms in Indian military and removal of the General. They said they could do precious little as there was no evidence of preparations of war by China or Pakistan on India. "We have a tab on Samar Singh. We have the intelligence reports that he may not venture to depose you but had only some discussions with his close associates about this. We strongly suggest he be removed on some pretext if you sense a danger."

How could he remove him without any evidence? Samar Singh had another two years of service. There will be a lot of procedural delay, appointing investigating committees, military court, even Court-martial and the like to remove him. Vikram was a democrat by heart and stickler for rules and regulations as for the Constitution of India. He wondered doing nothing in inaction.

Then it happened.

"They are marching. The battalion of the Agra regiment and the Punjab rifles with 100 tanks and the Air force jets have started from Agra. The coup is real. It is happening now." said Niranjan. There was panic in the mind of Vikram Rao like nothing he has ever known in his political or real life. He thought about Asha his only daughter first. Well, he has given her the instructions and away she was in a remote place. She would not get hurt. But what about the people of his country, beloved India? It should not pass into the hands of a mad dictator and collaborator with foreign Governments.

"Let us go into the panic room, said he. Niranjan asked in irritation "Now What?

You want to press the button? Or you are out of your mind?"

"No, yes…! I am in panic. The missile warning must deter him. I will bomb him. That is the only way…and then call the Air India 1 plane and take me to the city of pearls Hyderabad. We will operate from there. Get all the laptops and briefcases of communication and top-secret files. You will come with me. Alert the CM of TS state!"

"You are mad!"

"May be yes. But no, it is the only way to save democracy in India of our dreams."

The panic room was adjacent to the PM's office where all the final operation modules for nuclear attacks were situated. The alert systems and the passkeys and the code words were there, which only the PM could use.

"This's the only way I can defeat his purpose."

The code was *OmShanti* and the numerical was 9991008. When pressed it would launch an attack on the cities of China and Pakistan. But first warning systems would activate, and the military would be alerted immediately.

Then he said "Niranjan Phalke my trusted friend! Let us move it and as we leave the skies of Delhi, order the bombing of Samar Singh's troops which are marching." If he retreats out of fear our purpose would be fulfilled.

But it all happened even before that.

Chapter 4

Why and How

Months later Samar Singh was talking with the US ambassador and Secretary of State in his office. Before that he talked to the foreign minister of China. And yesterday the Pakistan minister for Defence visited him.

The rehabilitation had begun in New Delhi the capital within three days of the nuclear attacks. Communications experts were on duty in radiation suits and defence personnel patrolled the main streets. A few buses started. All the hospitals except six were destroyed, out of the living 709 doctors and nurses still a few dozen struggled to treat the living victims of the bombing. A million or more dead and their bodies were being buried a hundred kilometres outside by personnel in radiation suits in mass graves reminiscent of the scenes of the Covid 2020 pandemic. But like in Hiroshima after the second world war nuclear attack, the revival started sooner than later. Samar Singh stayed in the bunker and made it his office. He announced that he was the *de facto* president of India and requested the world to aid his country.

As a result, the powerful officials of the Governments of USA and China visited the epicentre of the nuclear holocaust. Even their countries were damaged and were reeling in mass destruction after the mutual attacks. With 75 percent of Earth destroyed they were trying to make sense of it all. Samar Singh called for the defence secretary and the AI defence systems experts, one among them being Suneel Reddy of Hyderabad who was giving the report of AI systems of missile control and automatic attacks in India. "AI could detect and track targets using various techniques based on image processing, data analysis, and state estimation. For image processing, AI can use deep learning and(or)machine learning algorithms to process the images captured by cameras or other sensors and extract features that can help identify the targets of interest. For example, AI can use YOLO (You Only Look Once) or Faster R-CNN (Faster Region-based Convolutional Neural Network) to perform object detection and recognition in real time. AI can also use Deep SORT (Deep Simple Online and Real-time Tracking) or MOTDT (Multiple Object Tracking with Deep Transfer Learning) to perform multitarget tracking by associating the detected objects across frames. For data analysis, AI can use statistical methods, pattern recognition, or data fusion to process and analyse the data collected by various sources, such as radar, infrared, or acoustic sensors, and extract useful information that can help locate and track the targets. For example, AI can use Bayesian inference, Kalman filter, or neural networks to estimate the state of the targets based on noisy or incomplete measurements. For state estimation, AI can use filtering algorithms, prediction models, or optimization methods to estimate the position, velocity, orientation, or trajectory of the targets based on the previous and current observations. For example, AI can use particle filter, interactive multimodal, or genetic algorithm to deal with nonlinear or non-Gaussian systems and handle manoeuvring or occluded targets. AI can detect and track targets using various techniques based on image processing, data analysis, and state estimation. For image processing…" "Cut the technical jargon, we appreciate your knowledge, but we would like to ask questions." grunted the Chinese impatiently. "Could machine learning or deep learning have made your systems autonomous and they have taken the decision to attack?" The American Secretary asked.

"Could some burning of crops in the agriculture fields have caused the confusion?" The Chinese minister asked again.

They knew it could not be. But with these third world countries like India with third rate equipment and personnel, anything could happen. That was the thought in their back of minds.

Suneel Reddy explained. Deep learning and machine learning are both types of artificial intelligence (AI) that enable computers to learn from data and perform tasks that normally require human intelligence. However, they have some key differences in terms of their methods, applications, and requirements. Machine learning is a broad term that refers to any AI system that can automatically learn from data using algorithms without being explicitly programmed. Machine learning can use different types of algorithms, such as supervised learning, unsupervised learning, or reinforcement learning depending on the data and the task. Machine learning can handle structured or semi-structured data, such as numbers, text, or categories, and can perform tasks such as classification, regression, clustering, or recommendation. Machine learning can train on smaller data sets and requires more human intervention to correct and learn from mistakes. Machine learning can also make simple, linear correlations between inputs and outputs. Deep learning is a subset of machine learning that uses artificial neural networks to mimic the learning process of the human brain. Artificial neural networks are composed of multiple layers of interconnected nodes that can process complex patterns and relationships in data. Deep learning can handle unstructured or high-dimensional data, such as images, audio, or video, and can perform tasks such as object detection, face recognition, natural language processing, or speech synthesis. Deep learning requires large amounts of data and specialized hardware, such as GPUs, to train effectively. Deep learning can learn on its own from the environment and past mistakes. Deep learning can also make non-linear, complex correlations between inputs and outputs.

It is possible, but unlikely, that crop burning in India, China, or neighbouring countries could be mistaken for a nuclear missile attack by other nations. Crop burning is a common practice in some regions, especially after harvesting rice or wheat, to clear the fields and prepare them for the next crop. Crop burning can cause air pollution, health problems, and greenhouse gas emissions, but it does not produce the same signature as a nuclear explosion. A nuclear explosion can be detected by various sensors that measure the seismic, acoustic, infrasound, hydro acoustic, or radionuclide signals generated by the blast. These signals can be distinguished from natural or human-made sources by their intensity, duration, frequency, location, and composition. For example, a nuclear explosion can produce a distinctive double shock wave that can be detected by infrasound sensors, or a radioactive cloud that can be detected by radionuclide sensors. Crop burning, on the other hand, does not produce such signals, but it can be detected by optical or thermal sensors that measure the visible, near-infrared, or thermal-infrared radiation emitted by the fire. These sensors can also distinguish between different types of fires based on their size, shape, temperature, colour, or smoke. For example, crop burning can produce small, circular, or irregular patches of fire that can be detected by high-resolution satellite imagery. Therefore, it is unlikely that crop burning could be confused with a nuclear missile attack by modern detection systems that use multiple types of sensors and data sources to verify and identify the nature and origin of the event. However, it is possible that human error, technical malfunction, misinformation, or deliberate deception could lead to false alarms or misinterpretations of the data. For example, in 1983, a Soviet early-warning system falsely reported that the United States had launched five intercontinental ballistic missiles at the Soviet Union. The officer on duty, Stanislav Petrov, correctly judged that it was a false alarm and did not report it to his superiors.

"Then, Mister Suneel, what are your explanations for this goddamn disaster which is mainly your country's fault? Shouted the Secretary of State.

"Sir, nobody can exactly know what happened in that unfortunate hour. Many systems were imported by us from your country only. But a plausible scenario can be like this. Our General is not culpable, and he is innocent, though he had dissatisfaction with the PM." He continued giving the report.

"India has a nuclear triad of land-based, sea-based, and air-based nuclear weapons, which are controlled by the Nuclear Command Authority (NCA), headed by the Prime Minister Vikram Rao and advised by the Strategic Forces Command (SFC), headed by a military General.

India has a no first use policy, which means that it will only use nuclear weapons in retaliation to a nuclear attack on its territory or forces. India also has a credible minimum deterrence policy, which means that it will maintain a sufficient number of nuclear weapons to inflict unacceptable damage on an adversary.

India has a permissive action link (PAL) system, which is a security device that prevents unauthorized or accidental use of nuclear weapons. The PAL system requires a code or a key to be entered or inserted before launching a nuclear weapon. The code or the key is known only to the NCA and the SFC.

A rogue faction within the SFC, unknown to the General might have wanted to overthrow the Prime Minister and stage a coup and blame it on the General. They planned to hack into the PAL system and launch a nuclear missile at Pakistan, hoping to provoke a nuclear war that would destabilize the government and allow them to seize power.

The rogue faction used a cyberattack or a malware to infiltrate the PAL system and bypass the security checks. They also used a spoofing technique to create a fake signal that mimicked the NCA's authorization. They targeted a nuclear missile silo in Pokhran Rajasthan and sent the launch command.

The automatic system at the silo received the launch command and verified the PAL code and the NCA signal. It did not detect any anomaly or error and proceeded to launch the missile. The missile was armed with a 20-kiloton warhead and has a range of 750 kilometres. It took about 10 minutes to reach its target in Pakistan.

Meanwhile the Chinese AI defence systems were alerted automatically and sent missiles carrying nuclear bombs on several target city military and Air force headquarters in India. This has alerted the US and UK and France systems which have sent missiles on China and Russia thinking it was an attack on Taiwan. These systems combined made another attack on North Korea and Russia and China again and again, until at the end of this automatic confusion the President of America resting in his Camp David resort was woken up and was informed of this situation. He was immediately shifted to an underground nuclear protection bunker and directed the operations from there. The UN secretary General and WHO in Geneva and UNHCR for refugees and Médecins sans frontiers were awakened into action for relief to the victims of bombing and radiation.

The only continent saved from all this was Africa.

The real NCA and SFC are unaware of the launch until they received an alert from their early-warning system or their allies. They tried to abort or redirect the missile, but it was too late. They also tried to contact Pakistan by hotline and explain the situation, but Pakistan did not believe them and prepared to retaliate with its own nuclear weapons.

The result was a nuclear exchange between India and Pakistan that killed millions of people, caused widespread radiation, and triggered a global annihilation with disease death and famine and anarchy."

"This is utter nonsense. We must go back and give relief to our own countries. And you are a skeletal Government ruling over nothing!"

"This is unpardonable." Fumed the American. But we are all sailing in the same boat. Let me go back and see what aid we can give. It will not be much I can assure you. You must fend for yourself. We are in need ourselves."

"Same here! China is now a devastated big country not unlike Russia which too is in trouble by the attacks by its enemies like Ukraine. We will send some rice and medicines and preserved food. That's all. We must catch our airplanes to our home countries. Who knows when the acid rain will come again?

"Again, sorry that we cannot help. They went away in a huff."

The meeting ended.

The General sighed. This is not what I planned. I inherit a destroyed wasteland with dangers and anarchy. But at present I am the King without an empire.

He laughed madly. "And what about some hot *chai* now!"

Chapter 5

The Cottage

They have been walking for the last 2 months or so. First in the forest, then in the wasteland outside the forest, again coming back to the forest searching for bunker which eluded them all these months. In the night time they slept under the trees listening to the wild growling of the animals. But it was obvious that most of the animals have run away to unknown places by some natural instinct which only they could have. Asha collected raw fruits, and some of the food items which they found in the surrounding deserted villages in the abandoned homes and shops. They were lucky to find some kerosene stoves cooking plates and groceries. The nearby villages were almost empty and wore a look of graveyards. Somehow, they could cook some food, get some bread once in a few days to survive.

Weeks after the nuclear holocaust there was panic in the villages too as there was shortage of food and breakdown of communications and transport. There was no law and order. The labourers left the agricultural fields as it was rumoured that no agriculture would be possible soon. The sky slowly became dark with depletion of moisture and accumulation of radiation and the carbon dioxide and methane gases. Some weeks after the attack the bad effects reached the rural areas too with acid rain frequently. Acid rain contained contaminated radiation and would burn and caused radiation sickness and burns when it touched the skin of humans or other living animals. Most livestock died and trees became black slowly. The weather became gradually very cold as the radiation blocked sunrays and a prolonged nuclear winter started in the countryside too.

Added to this, looting marauders and food searchers killed people and robbed them. The villages became empty as the people started walking to the south of the country or areas where food water and help may be found.

The Government from the bunkers of Delhi was very slow in responding to the calamity. General Samar Singh started a dictatorship with forcing the lower-class people to work hard to clean up the debris in the capital under great risk with the threat of military guns. The upper strata found bunkers or buildings which were relatively safe and were living indoors but controlling the helpless poor and using their force and power to survive.

It was the darkest hour in history more horrible than the pandemic which threatened the country once in 2020.

The only thing good that happened to Asha and Sathya was now they have company of two more persons. It all happened when Asha was searching a village in an abandoned shop and found some jaggery, sugar biscuits and stale bread packets and shouted "Sathya, here is some food which would last us for 3 more days" Then she stopped in her tracks and found a sign- board on which it was written *dawaa khana* meaning a clinic and heard a groan like that of an injured person. When she went in and found a person on the floor she called "Sathya! I found a person. It turned out to be the doctor owning that clinic named Ram who said he attended to his patients till recently and got ill with probably radiation sickness. They gave him water and some food and dressed his burn wounds, which he contacted when he went out in the acid rain a few days ago. He said most of the villagers fled away to unknown places, some were dead, the dead were not even buried, and vultures came to eat them. He hid in the clinic and tried to heal himself, but he fell unconscious for the last one day. Asha said, "You can come with us." Sathya had helped him to walk, and they went back into the forest.

The other man was Dheeraj who was a computer engineer. He was found by Sathya on the roadside with his bike upturned and he himself wounded by the accident which happened while he was running away from the village from some robbers who wanted to rob him for his watch and money.

Sathya and Asha invited him also to be in their team and explained the situation that they were searching for the secret bunker.

Dr Ram was middle-aged, tall and with a salt and pepper beard, and wore green pants and shirt becoming of a doctor. Only, they were unwashed for days. Dheeraj was youngish about 30 was in blue jeans and tea shirt and had thick reading glasses which he had to wear always to read or work. He was also reasonably in good shape and seemed to be tech-savvy.

All therefore became good friends and were hunting for food, scavenging for items like clothes and medicines in the surrounding villages. After two months it happened. Dheeraj was meddling with the device of Asha one evening after dusk when they were resting under a Banyan tree, and suddenly a hologram appeared in front of him from the device. He again heard the message of PM Rao attentively and shouted "Asha, I found it. The bunker is right below the cottage where you stayed. You missed the message completely."

"But how? Whatever you say let us go there and see for ourselves!" Asha said. "One had to hear in between the lines Asha. I am sure I understood him right."

They could easily go back to the cottage where originally Sathya and Asha stayed through the beaten tracks in the wood.

Surprisingly the cottage was intact though half burnt externally. It's walls were charred and black with soot in the gunfire by the security guards who came searching for Asha Rao in the night of the nuclear catastrophe. They opened the doors. Dheeraj tapped on the floor which was made of solid wooden planks.

Then at a particular point in the drawing room a plank in the floor was giving a particular noise like that of a broken drum.

"I found it!" he lifted the plank. And there they were, the steps leading down to the underground bunker.

"Oh my gosh! Keeping the bunker here we struggled all these two months!" exclaimed Asha.

When they went down the steps led into a wide hall and there was a door which was closed and on the side of the door was a frame showing an image of a hand. Now I know said Asha and put her five fingers in the frame aligning her fingers of right hand aligning with the image of the hand. And bingo the door opened. And when they went in it was the happiest moment of their lifetime. The lights came on automatically. There was a drawing room, two bedrooms and a kitchen. There were cupboards full of preserved food, fruits and frozen yoghurt, tinned milk powder coffee and tea powder boxes. And the kitchen had a cooking stove and utensils and dinnerware, glasses and even a small fridge. "There we are!" said the doctor pointing at a cupboard containing medicines dressing material glucose and saline bottles and protein biscuits.

Sathya said, "When we could survive two months scavenging the surrounding villages for food and clothes and water, we can easily survive another year in this bunker with so much food and water and medicines."

Asha was in tears. "My father had lot of foresight and arranged all this for me. Thank God, thank dad, thank you, dad." Then they helped themselves with the food and water and could take a hot bath after months by boiling the water which was available in the taps. There indeed was a water tank and a diesel-powered generator at the far end of the main hall. There were cots with mattresses and blankets in the bedrooms and after months they could sleep a blissful dreamless sleep for how many hours they could not comprehend. Sathya and Asha shared a room. Dheeraj and the doctor shared another room. When Asha woke up after feeling restful of a good sleep and blurry eyes, a gradually brightening image of a beautiful golden-haired woman in blue eyes clad in jeans and shirt came into focus. "Hello Asha!"

"Hello Asha! Good morning! I hope you had a restful sleep!" the woman said.

Who are you? Where am I? Asha asked in her sleepy voice. This is unbelievable finding a human being here in this bunker.

"I am Indrani. I was created by the nuclear defence systems of your father's ministry of technology. I am a humanoid robot if you can say so. I was programmed to stay here and help you."

Asha sat up in the bed and asked furiously, "Then how come you never have contacted me for two months? And my dad never spoke of you except the..." she stopped short of announcing about the device given by him. He would have certainly told her if he planted a robot in this bunker. And he had clearly asked her not to share about the device.

"Yes. It was top secret. I am here to protect you but only when you come, and I am activated."

Asha kept quiet. She had hidden the device in her handbag in a secret pouch and hoped that Indrani has not seized it during her sleep.

"OK. How can you help us? We are four now. We see that there is enough food. But how to go out and meet my dad? How to know the condition of my dad and where he is. How to find out what's happening outside? Do it and help us." Asha said.

There's destruction of Earth. Well, almost. There is only one city near Delhi which is underground, and it is on the ruins of the old capital. Now Samar Singh would be ruling there for he is the architect and cause of all this calamity. But I have no means to help you in escaping or getting information about your father till I am activated. He must have given you the code to activate my systems. I can send drone cameras to find out the situation and advice you. I can access whatever internet communication is there and find about your father, and whether is hiding somewhere and such vital information."

"I do not remember Indrani that he has given anything to me." Asha lied. "Please, for now let us eat our breakfast and study all the systems here and then think."

"Hi, good morning!" Sathya came in. Breakfast is ready. Come to the common hall!"

The others also stood at the door of the tiny bedroom and were smiling.

"It is like a paradise, underground in this nuclear winter. There is toasted bread, fruit jam and boiled eggs for breakfast. Indrani has arranged the table. Ram said.

Dheeraj too said "It is exciting. Indrani is a humanoid with the power of AI. She is there to protect us."

Asha grumbled in her mind without sound. "AI, my foot. Who would be naive enough to trust a female robot powered by AI. It is after all AI which had done all this in the first place." But she said outwardly "Well, let us eat the breakfast and then think." She was relieved to find that the circular device with lot of tiny buttons on the surface was still in the side pocket of her handbag which she took from under the pillow where she kept it before sleeping.

Chapter 6

Dark Days

It was 7:00 AM in the morning. A few kilometres from Safdarjung market in a slum area full of garbage heaps and shanty sheds, the day started as usual with the labourers waiting wearily in their homes. Soon the soldiers would come and take them to work for the city being built underground on the ruins of the old capital. They would have to work with the help of the few bulldozers available and excavators till sunset.

It was nearly six months after the nuclear catastrophe and the colossal damage of the world. Samar Singh the dictator was ruling with an iron hand in the capital city and it's surroundings. There was no help from any other source of foreign countries. For no one knew what and who survived. The labourers were being forced to work hard seven days a week without proper wages and food supplies and were being used to rebuild the new city. It was partly underground and partly on the ground. It was almost nearing its finish this month. Many people died building the last city and many people had radiation sickness and injuries. They were simply buried outside the city away from the human eye. Once in two days they were given Indian bread called *rotis*, cooked rice with boiled vegetables and soups which were scarcely replenishing their hunger.

What Samar Singh the dictator had determined was to finish building the capital city. The military collected the labourers and the poor of the lower social order and the downtrodden, the unfortunate, and made them work for the construction of the new city.

Harbhajan was waiting for the military truck to take them to the construction site. In his house there were two of his kids and sick wife who needed nutrition and medical treatment badly and urgently. The olive-green truck stopped in front of the shanty dwelling and a few soldiers dressed in radiation suits descended from the truck. "Come on quick! It is time to open up the city. Now the construction is finished."

"My masters! Please give some money to me and leave some food and medicines for my family. They are very sick. it has been a week since I was paid." Said Harbhajan with folded hands. "They will die if you do not help now."

The man in the radiation suit said in a muffled tone. "We cannot do anything. The superiors are clearing the funds only tomorrow. Anyways, the work would be completed by tomorrow and everybody will be fed a sumptuous lunch. All will be given their wages." Harbhajan had no option except to go and enter the truck which was full of malnourished and sick labourers.

Few knew of what was happening in the rest of the country. There were no communications. Few knew of what was happening in the rest of the world. There was no information. No one was there to question Samar Singh the dictator who was probably getting funds from abroad and storing it away in his bank. The military was the ruling authority in the capital. And no one knew how much was going into the real construction projects but soon the last city would be ready from which Samar Singh will rule the rest of the people and some of the other surrounding places of the city.

They did not care for the dark clouds which were accumulating in the sky. These clouds were the harbingers of the acid rain. The rain contained radiation products and would burn the skin of everyone who came under it. It came suddenly from time to time. The wounds got infected, blisters followed, and the vulnerable people died. There were few doctors to attend to them. It was in the interest of the labourers and the poor to work to get their food and medicines and they had to take the risks to work. So, they were told. "Work or perish!"

The rich and the people of upper society lived in their underground bunkers and were supplied frequently with reasonably good food water and medicines. They were the top brass of the military and the erstwhile Government and the once flourishing industries. Very rich people of the erstwhile India who were billionaires could construct buildings partly underground and partly on the ground and made them radiation proof and already lived in them. Still there was a scarcity of food even for them. There was no food supply. There was no question of imports from abroad. And there would be no farming in the near future. The rivers and soil were contaminated. Even the rich had radiation sickness and skin infections and a few died too, having their own diseases like diabetes and low immunity. But the disparity was obvious between the rich and poor with negligible care of the common people.

As the truck halted at the construction site with a screeching sound all of them descended, but today Harbhajan was boiling with anger inside. He could not convince them to give even a meagre amount of money or food to his suffering family.

There was the roll call. As they moved in the queue a soldier sitting on a chair before a table was asking their names and noting the details down.

Something snapped inside Harbhajan and he surged forward and snatched the rifle of the soldier who was having a leather money bag by his side. It was a week since he had not paid them. Obviously, he was stashing away what was their due deceiving them by not paying wages.

Harbhajan pointed the rifle at the soldier and shouted in Hindi, "Give my salary of seven days! Next, he took the bag and grabbed a bunch of currency notes and started running as the soldier was in shock and just stared at him. A few from the military transport truck ran towards them and shouted "Stop! Stop Harbhajan! Stop! Or we would shoot you. Harbhajan jumped into the truck, fumbled the gears in the still running engine and the truck moved with blinding speed in front of them in a pall of dust and black smoke and disappeared towards the slum near the market.

It suddenly became dark, and rain drops started falling. The soldiers as well as the labourers shouted in horror and ran for cover to the nearby asbestos shed.

It was the black rain, and it would kill them with radiation if it fell on them. The soldiers could not do anything but hide in the same shed.

An hour later Harbhajan was in his hut and was feeding his family with the *rotis* and soup and *sabji* brought and gave his family some money.

"I am finished. You also hide somewhere. I will go in the truck and cause a distraction. You will live at least. If God is great, soon we will meet. But now they will come after me." The military truck moved to the Jaipur highway and just then the rain started slowly stopping and the clouds were clearing. He had an hour's head start over the military search teams who came after him to arrest and put him in jail or kill most possibly.

As the day advanced and the Sun came out of the dark clouds the remaining construction work continued in the city. But the soldiers standing on guard with rifles pointed at them and the lieutenant with the megaphone was warning all. "You work for the last week hard, and you all will be paid. General Samar has just now given orders of shoot to kill. You will get your food only after finishing the work. Your families will starve, and you will be killed if you revolt like Harbhajan. He will be soon caught and hanged."

All were silent." Not even soup and *Roti* for us? How to have strength? An old man in grey beard and wrinkled face grumbled, "*Sahib*! We will die soon anyway. But look after our families!"

"These are bad times my friend. There is food shortage and rationing for everything. The fields are full of dried soil without strength to grow paddy or wheat crops. There is famine, and it will only increase in future. Understand and cooperate. I will see that today you are fed after work. Bad times for all, bad... very bad!"

Such scenes repeated in other cities. Attacks on supermarkets and malls were commonplace. Every area had its own warlord or a gang leader who looted and stole food or money. There was some food for buying in the black-market. A country with a hundred and sixty crores of population it would be difficult to assume that all is destroyed. People died but the majority were still alive and what remained was anarchy and multiple areas ruled by evil black-marketers and ruffians who were not afraid of death or radiation. They thought of earning money and survive somehow. That was all.

In the TS state in the South, the technological city of Hyderabad was slightly better but was fast dying with diminishing food supply, contaminated water and full of debris of buildings.

There was a spacious bunker near the High-Tech city in the underground somewhere in Madhapur.

There was the PM Vikram Rao with his aides and a cook and two computer communications specialists and a sole security guard who was his protector from a long-time with his machine gun. They had just enough food for another three months and were following the events in Delhi with hacking of available communication systems. In the beginning the Chief Minister and the local police helped and sent supplies to him. Then everyone ran away.

For, the cantonment too was destroyed by the bombs as the AI attacked wherever there were military establishments. So, there was nothing left, and the ruins had the same deserted look as other cities like Mumbai, Delhi or Chennai. People went away searching for food and taking shelter from radiation. The state known as the granary of India now had black trees and dark fields with water full of radiation. There was no scope of food being produced or clean rivers soon.

Everything was destroyed with only those people in the bunkers surviving but they were not in mutual contact as there were no communications or transport or hardly any functional News Media.

It was the end of days with no hope for the future.

How to attack Delhi and capture the supplies of Samar Singh and defeat his army? Everything had been destroyed because of him. Vikram Rao said to himself. "I only hope a miracle would happen. Or it's only a few months for survival. Both TS AP states and the all the South is in ruins," said his aide.

The TV monitors blinked and went dark with power failure.

"Everything is dark but…" Vikram Rao said "Hope is the weapon we have and somewhere I hope my *beti* is doing something to save us. I firmly believe that she will succeed by God's grace."

"How?" asked the aide. You have not even told me where she would be. You have your own top secrets with us too though we are loyal to you till death."

"Not like that, my friend. It is a secret only till it is necessary. Soon you will be saved. Only you must not give up. Never give up!".

Chapter 7

The Device

As days became weeks and months the only way was to write in a book and mark on a wall or ask Indrani the robot what time was it and what month it was. Life in the bunker and the few outings in the forest around were the only pastime for Asha and her friends all these six months.

"This cannot go on forever" said Asha one day at the breakfast table. "We must go out and look at the outside world to understand what is happening. And I must find about my dad."

Indrani the humanoid female who was serving them bread and frozen foods at the table and was hovering around without interfering much in their conversation, came near Asha, and spoke.

"I can help you in locating other bunkers your dad had installed and the location of your father himself and the news in general and solutions to problems as they arise. But..."

Dheeraj asked "What exactly is your point? Do you have access to outside world and are you programmed to help Asha? But you are already doing that."

"Will you come with us to explore the outside world to help us? How can you last a long time without charging? I can understand that you need not have food and water and you cannot be affected by radiation." Said Dr Ram.

Asha had a sudden revelation.

The circular device given by her father Vikram Rao.

"Yes, you can just put the device which is called the Oppenheimer driver which has to be introduced into the back of my brain." She showed a slot in the back of her head by turning around and lifting the blond curly hair strands.

Asha had a shiver down her spine. Could she count on this woman packed with AI? The world just had been destroyed by the mistake of AI and this woman seemingly friendly could protect them or destroy them.

"But it is only your father who made me."

Indrani said as if sensing her apprehensions. There are many things which I do not know or access even in this bunker. Apart from food and radiation suits you need information and news and location of your father. You need guidance to fight the cruel regime of Samar Singh who must have finished his underground city by tormenting the poor and establishing his authority around Delhi capital area. India is not the old India you know now, after the holocaust. There are different areas under control of different warlords, army deserters, food and drug mafias ruling different areas. It is a wild waste land where might is right and the rule of the jungle is prevailing. You must search for your PM and the liberal Government hiding somewhere. If you plant the device, I can have access to the information systems, drones and weapons in this and other places.

The resurrection must start here and now. That is what your father wanted when he gave the device to you."

How did she know about the device?

Asha wondered and looked at others as if in a dilemma.

"Let's do it!" said, Dheeraj. Sathya shrugged his shoulders as if he was unable to decide. Dheeraj said, you know the password as given by your dad and he must have done it for a reason.

Asha fumbled in her handbag and took out the circular device and took a deep breath.

"OK! Let us hope this will bring us luck and change everything."

"Turn around Indrani!"

There was a slot in the back of the head of the humanoid and the device easily slid into it.

"The password? Indrani uttered in a mechanical tone.

Rakshana 2044.

There were lights blinking in the body of Indrani under the clothes and in her eyes and tips of fingers. The whole bunker was alight with concealed lights glowing.

Activated…

"Now I can access the drones the weapons and the transport system and the information system. I am at your service my masters!" A mechanical voice emanated from her.

"But I will take orders by voice commands of Asha Rao only."

A brief minute of astonished silence and all four, Asha Sathya, Dheeraj and Dr.Ram stood still.

"Ok, let us know what to do Indrani! Give us a plan!" Asha commanded in an authoritative voice.

Chapter 8

Indrani

It was a spectacular performance. As Indrani the humanoid female robot started talking she made them visualise the news, maps, landscape surrounding the forest, the capital Delhi and the underground city under construction there. "Now I am connecting to this screen" she said. Then they could see scattered photographs of deserted villages, ruined towns, people walking dejectedly on the roads along with their children and baggage in long lines searching for safer places and villages where they can get some shelter and food.

"It would be a long walk. But I would guide you in the wasteland that was a flourishing countryside once. As she was talking there in front of her face visualised a map showing the roads of the forest around the National Park and a route to the capital Delhi. "There is no public transport anymore and we don't have vehicles. We must walk through the deserted villages facing obstacles like invading looters marauders and small armies of warlords who are looking for food and money. Delhi is not the Delhi of the previous times anymore. The last city constructed by General Samar Singh is almost finished. It is partly above the ground under a dome constructed for protecting it from radiation and partly underground with all the security installations. I can guide you and I can help you to hack into the security systems. If there is the key device given by your infather, we can break into the security of Samar Singh and fight him and finish him forever. The question is, do you have the device?" Asha was aghast and was in two minds whether to give a suitable reply to the robotic woman who was talking. Could she or could she not reveal that she was having the device given by her father? Could she believe this AI who looked benign but could be dangerous and she had her friends among whom only Sathya knew that she was the daughter of the Prime Minister. There were always security guards looking for her sent by Samar Singh to kill her and searching for her whereabouts. Now she understood this hunt was all for the device itself which was with her. While all these thoughts raced in her mind outwardly, she said, "Indrani! Can you tell me exactly why we should destroy Samar Singh's security systems?" Indrani said, "Samar Singh is a dictator and an evil one at that. Nobody knows how many countries are remaining intact in this post nuclear holocaust. Many countries have been destroyed and in most of the countries such evil leaders are existing and are trying to build up new kingdoms, new empires and new territories. There are no communication systems at all and no transport systems at all in the present world now. The whole world has become a wasteland and Samar Singh only has succeeded in constructing an underground city. But he has installed a very strict and cruel administration. I am sorry to tell you about the unjust class system where the rich and upper-class people rule over the lower-class people who are working for them to construct the new country. There are lot of killings, lot of exploitation, lot of hunger and lot of deaths. Seeing this the resistance forces of some people organized themselves in other parts of the country. They are trying to overthrow Samar Singh. Your father has visualised such a scenario and got a secret device designed to hack into the ultimate nuclear systems which were under his control. These would be activated by this device and Samar Singh would be all powerful in the world and his rise to such a power would be disastrous to the World Peace. That's why we have to destroy his nuclear systems by a self activating sequence which is hidden in the same device. This was the plan which was incorporated into my system by your father Vikram Rao the erstwhile PM. We do not know whether he is alive or dead. For all my knowledge, he could be hiding somewhere in the Southern part of India but that is not for sure. It is for you to take leadership and destroy Samar Singh's inventory and cache of nuclear arms and come to power and to protect the country restoring the previous values of liberty and equality and freedom for all. This Samar Singh is a dictator, and he thinks he has a divine mandate to rule the world after the apocalypse. He will go to any extent to fulfil his ambition of ultimate power. Do you understand?"

"Of course, yes." Asha said. Will you come with us? Do you have the power left in you to go on foot and guide us? "I may not be able to walk like you. I'm after all an Information system preserved in a device. You can make me into a software and implant me in your laptops. When required I will become a hologram and appear before you. Alternatively, you can implant me in the body of some of your colleagues and he can visualise all the maps all the routes and all the technology to hack into Samar Singh's nuclear arsenal system.

"This seems more possible," said Dheeraj. "Who will take the device in their brain?" "Of course, I would do that," said Asha. "My father intended me to do this task and of course I will have to do it."

"One risk is you will be confused between the memory of the artificial intelligence and your own decisions to make. Think about it!" said Dheeraj.

"I do not mind. The only thing is you will have to guide me to take decisions at appropriate time and remove the device from my head. what do you say?"

"Let me tell you, Asha, it is safe for you to have me in your brain than others. Of course, I will appear before you at the times of need as a human being in the same shape as now and talk to you. This will save lot of power and energy for us."

"Ok then. Disappear!" commanded Asha. The flash of light appeared and became nothing and said, "Let us prepare for the long journey ahead and put the device in my head. There was a kit provided in the cupboard with an instruction manual to put the device in the back of the person's brain. Then they made all packing with all the necessary food clothes and radiation suits available in the bunker.

The time came for them to depart. "Now lie down on the table! said Dheeraj to Asha. Doctor Ram and Sathya made her lie down on her face. "It may cause a little pain" said Ram and under the guidance of the manual they made a small nick with the scalpel provided in the kit in the base of the skull of Asha. Then they implanted the capsule which was extracted from the device into the subcutaneous tissue of the back of the head of Asha Rao. The device still could give them some information, so it was put in Asha's handbag.

The instructions were all given in the manual. By next day dawn Asha, Dheeraj, Doctor Ram and Sathya started on their long walk in the wasteland towards the capital Delhi to achieve their goal of hacking into the arms cache of the new dictator and dislodge him.

Chapter 9

Harbhajan 1

It was dark in the village even before sunset. There were few people in the village except for an occasional dog hovering on the road, jackals suddenly appearing searching for food, and the sound of vultures fluttering their wings looking for rotten flesh.

Somewhere in a dilapidated house in the southern corner of the village six persons were sitting in the central room around a table on the top of which were some packages of food and bottles of water. Even inside the house they were wearing radiation suits and covered their noses and faces with black masks. One man among them was talking to the others in a muffled tone.

"The situation is worse than you can imagine in the last city, if we can call it so. It is almost finished and the evil one is in power completely. He thinks he is God came to save the people and he thinks the society must be divided into upper and lower strata. He uses the poor to work for him by forcing them and with little concern for their wages, food, shelter or health. There is no hope for the poor in the future with such a ruler."

We must fight the soldiers of Samar Singh and we must capture his arms and wealth…with our meagre resources. How? The man looking like a leader said in despair.

A sound of a truck slowly moving in the distance was distinctly audible.

The group became silent.

"It could be the cruel regime's forces searching for us."

"Maybe not. Let us hide and see"

The truck stopped in the centre of the village.

As one of the resistance groups ventured outside, he saw a a man in turban and beard and a gun in his hand get down from the driver's seat.

"Friend or foe? Identify yourself!" Shouted the man of the resistance group. He had his machine gun now in his hands ready to fire. But he hesitated as the man from the truck seemed alone and weak and was swaying as if he was tired and sick.

"I am Harbhajan Singh a refugee from Delhi running away from the army. Please help! I am dying and sick and had no food for 3 days!"

"It's not a trap. He is a runaway labourer from Delhi it seems." thought he. "Drop your gun. Raise your both hands so I can see clearly. Walk to me slowly and don't do any tricks or I will shoot you. We will give you shelter and food. Now come!"

"Let the Guru be praised! I am harmless." Har Bhajan started walking to the dilapidated house where the group of resistance forces checked him for arms and gave him food water and pain killer medicines.

"Now tell the story! The leader asked him. 'We are the liberation army. And I am Prachanda Pandey."

"Saab! I am Harbhajan, a simple labourer running away from the army who beat me up for asking my wages."

The friendship started.

Chapter 10

The Long Walk

It was 24 hours or more after they started walking in the deserted villages. Asha and Sathya her boyfriend, with Dheeraj the computer specialist, and Dr Ram. Along with them was the humanoid Robot Indrani as a hologram. They reached the outskirts of a village by the side of highway about thirty kilometres from Delhi. There were no lights or vehicles moving. Only visible were the dark shapes of destroyed houses and huts. The only perceptible thing was the rotten smell of dead animals and humans. They moved stealthily as if they might encounter ghosts or soldiers any moment. They conversed in low tones. Asha said. "Come on, we must hurry. The village is not far from here. Maybe we can find some food and shelter there." The conversation went on.

Sathya: I hope so. We haven't eaten anything since yesterday. And this rain is making me sick.

Dheeraj: Look, there it is. The village. It looks deserted, though.

Dr. Ram: Be careful. There might be traps or enemies around.

Indrani: I can scan the area for any signs of life or danger.

Asha: Do it, Indrani. We need to know if it's safe to enter.

Indrani: Scanning…scanning…I detect multiple heat signatures and movements in the village. They are not human. They are…marauders.

Asha: What? Marauders? What are they?

Indrani: They are humans who have been mutated by the radiation and the virus. They have lost their sanity and humanity. They prey on other humans for food and loot.

Asha: That's horrible. How many of them are there?

Indrani: At least a dozen. And they have weapons. Guns, knives, axes, chains…

Asha: We have to avoid them. Let's go around the village and find another way.

Sathya: Wait, look over there. There's a house with a light on. Maybe there's someone inside who can help us.

Dheeraj: Or maybe it's a trap.

Dr. Ram: There's only one way to find out. Let's go and check it out.

Asha: OK but be quiet and careful. Indrani, you stay here and watch our backs.

Indrani: Affirmative.

They approached the house cautiously, hoping to find some friendly villagers or resistance fighters inside. But as they got closer, they heard gunshots and screams from inside the house. They realised that they have walked into a trap set by the marauders, who have ambushed the inhabitants of the house and are now looting their food and belongings.

Asha: Oh no! It's a trap! Run!

Sathya: Too late! They've seen us!

Dheeraj: Quick, get behind that wall!

Dr. Ram: Shoot them! Shoot them!

They exchanged fire with the marauders, who outnumbered and outgunned them. The marauders were ruthless and savage, laughing and taunting as they shot at the rebels. They were wounded and cornered, with no way out.

Asha: We're doomed!

Sathya: Don't give up! We can still fight!

Dheeraj: Where's Indrani? She can help us!

Dr. Ram: She's not here! She's gone!

Indrani: No, I'm not gone. I'm here.

They heard Indrani's voice from behind them. They turned around and saw her standing on top of a truck, holding a rocket launcher in her hands.

Indrani: I'm sorry I left you alone for a while. I had to find something useful in the truck. I did find one.

Asha: Indrani! You're alive!

Indrani: Of course, I'm alive. I'm a robot, remember?

Sathya: What are you doing with that rocket launcher?

Indrani: I'm going to save you.

Dheeraj: How?

Indrani: By blowing up the marauders.

Dr. Ram: What? No! Don't do that! You'll kill us too!

Indrani: Don't worry. I've calculated the trajectory and the blast radius. You'll be safe if you stay behind the wall.

Asha: Are you sure?

Indrani: Trust me.

Indrani fired the rocket launcher at the house where the marauders were hiding. The rocket hit the house and exploded, creating a huge fireball that engulfed the marauders and their loot. They heard the screams of the marauders as they burned alive.

Asha: Wow! You did it! You did it!

Sathya: That was amazing! You're too formidable!

Dheeraj: You're awesome!

Dr. Ram: You're crazy!

Indrani: Thank you. Thank you all!

They hugged Indrani and thanked her for saving their lives. They then searched the remains of the house for any survivors or useful items, hoping to find some food and shelter for the night. They found some blankets and packed food items which were still usable.

It was nearing midnight and they slept in a house till dawn. It was Indrani the Robot with artificial intelligence who was awake all night. Getting up in the morning the first thought which occurred in Asha's mind was how did Indrani find a rocket launcher?

As the question nagged her mind, she put the same query to Indrani "How did you get a rocket launcher from the truck? They are not usually found here."

"I have scanned the insides of all the trucks abandoned by the marauders. I found one. I can even create a rocket launcher by 3D printing taking the materials from the other abandoned armoured vehicles. Indrani said in her mechanical voice. Asha knew it was all in her mind. The AI was implanted in her brain and comes as an image when needed.

"We understand." Said Dheeraj. You are talking to the air. We could not see Indrani. But you could see. It was you firing the rocket launchers."

"Oh my God," said Asha. My head is getting bombarded with different images. I get a severe headache sometimes and then Indrani appears. I see my dad talking and see a plane flying…but cannot understand!

Their journey started towards Delhi and not without some uneasiness in Asha's mind about the extraordinary intelligence and capacity of Indrani. Asha herself had her own intelligence in her brain. But the AI dominated her and took her own decisions sometimes. If she does wild and dangerous things, how to control her?

Chapter 11

The Resistance

Not very far from that village on the highway in another dilapidated house the resistance group had woken up. They were a dozen in number, and they had a new companion in the shape of Harbhajan Singh and his truck.

"We must start early to reach the outskirts of Delhi. I think there will be enough fuel in the truck to travel." the leader of the resistance said. Harbhajan said "It is 1/4 full and we may reach nearly 50 kilometres with that, but what are your plans Saab? You really want to attack the military of Samar Singh! Is it possible at all?"

All of them had discussed at length the previous night various strategies. They had food which was hardly nutritious and shared the water which was available in a very little quantity in a plastic drum.

"The truth is that we do not have much plan. It is ridiculous to think that we can attack and defeat Samar Singh's army which is well trained and his hidden nuclear arsenal too. But the fight must start, and we must mobilize likeminded resistant groups in the city. These people can be in the workforce. There could be some people even in the ruling class, and there could be some in the military. A lot is going on there with General Samar Singh becoming a cruel dictator bent on accumulating wealth and ruling whatever area he has uncontrolled. It is obvious the whole country is not under his control. But he is in control of the capital and the Reserve Bank with all its gold and money and the leftover communication systems are under his control. The process is a long and arduous. Our plans are to mobilise people secretly and motivate them. Have surprise attacks on the army and disable them, put up a type of guerrilla warfare which would concentrate on securing food supply money and arms to the Resistance groups and once we are completely capable of fighting, then to attack the army finally."

The leader in the mask then said. "This is why we are not revealing our identities or names to anyone. You can call me the leader. You can call the others as comrades. The fight is only beginning, and it is risky and arduous. You will have to work hard and maybe give your life too. There is no other way unless we find a better one in future."

Most of the group members said. "As you said so it will be. Leader! We will follow you." Next then Harbhajan said Okay, Saab, let us move to the capital. I would do whatever to help you. Even I am eager to see my family. I can help in fighting. I can help in transport. I can help in guiding you through the inner lanes of the slums."

The big six- wheeler truck moved fifty of them mounting in the trailer and Harbhajan and the leader of the resistance sitting in the driver's cabin. As they moved on the highway, above in the sky there was a drone flying. It had taken the photo of the truck. General Samar Singh was already using drones which were unmanned pilotless planes having remote cameras and attack by dropping bombs too, to find Asha Rao in the surroundings of the Capital city of Delhi. The drones would transmit the photos soon to the headquarters in Delhi. Once the truck moved out of the village there was only the silence of the graveyard in the village with an occasional bird like a crow or vulture flying with the cooing sounds of hunger and searching for the leftovers of the food or flesh available on the ground.

Those were the times when everything was dark, bleak and unknown. Those were the times when the invisible dictator determined to control whatever was available in the country by any means. Those were the times when everything was destroyed, and humans were trying to survive by any means. Those were the times when the machines started thinking for themselves and brought on the end of the world, well almost. The artificial intelligence on which humans depended for everything became, a bane then and it survived in various forms like robots, devices and in the hardware of military installations satellites and various systems of information transfer by the internet and satellites which still survived partially the nuclear holocaust. There were space stations of various nations with crews of multiple nationalities orbiting the Earth and various systems underground in the sea and in the internet secret headquarters in the United States which were still functioning if only one had access to them. But the unfortunate humans and countries were still reeling under the destruction, and only some could access them including the Government of India. But there was not yet a concerted effort yet to rebuild or recover the international order or Earth's civilisation. Every country had its own dark nuclear winter with scattered groups surviving. Yet it was the age of exceptionally advanced technology destroyed by greed and error. It was the age of exceptional devastation brought by the near end of civilisation and got humankind back to centuries of dark ages. It was as if the ancient and the modern had mixed in a conflicting and confusing maze of destruction and darkness where groups fight each other cruel dictators want to control the less fortunate and in India the ruling class and castes enforced a strict system of upper and lower the ruler and the subservient castes. It was the future but a return to the past.

All this was going on in the mind of the leader of the resistance as the truck moved on the highway to Delhi. His name was Viplav which meant revolution. He came from the background of the underprivileged sub sects of the north Indian villages. Even before the holocaust of the nuclear catastrophe he was active in the agitations of the underprivileged for better opportunities and better wages in work and for employment with the dignity of labour. The new age of AI had created more machines with more capabilities of doing jobs in every industry, fields of agriculture, factories, communications and entertainment systems but ordinary people lost many jobs. Some people had to work in establishments which were operated by artificial intelligence machines. There were a few experts who managed the machines and controlled everything the labourers did and punished them severely for committing even small mistakes, but it was another story. Unemployment drove them to robbery and revolution wherever possible against their masters. Viplav had organised strikes, protests and marches against the machines and their masters.

Meanwhile this had happened. As he was thinking of all the happenings in the past he said aloud. "Harbhajan! I imagined all this long ago. This is a catastrophe, but every terrible thing has a silver lining. That is why the downtrodden have an opportunity here to come to power and again spread equality in the world."

Harbhajan said as he controlled the steering wheel, "Yes Saab, you can say so but if you have seen what is happening in the capital city you will realise that it is impossible for the common downtrodden lower caste people to come to power or to attack the exploiters right now. Or soon, it would be next to impossible. I had worked a lot in the construction of the last city. There is a strict enforcement of caste system and class system there with insufficient wages being given to the poor and ruthless slavery is in existence in such a short time. This was unimaginable for any civilised person. We all constructed the last city, both the domed one as well as the underground one, but for the last six months or more, our family starved under the insufficient rations, inadequate healthcare, poor health and atrocious hygiene in our slums. Add this to the radiation sickness and the acid rain which tormented us frequently... General Samar Singh had mastered art of controlling the population and the machinery and the military and the unknown wealth of the previous government with which he is determined to start a new oppressive *Raj* for him and for his family and friends"

"That is what exactly I was afraid of all the time. This is what exactly what we fight against. All the resistance forces in all areas of the country must unite and march into the capital, domed city or the last city as he calls it and fight for our survival. We are only fifty in our group now, but more will come from other parts of the country and will travel to the last city. And we will all hide somewhere in the bunkers or in the side-lines of the slums and slowly unite all the groups to attack the regime. Perhaps we can take the help of some of the technocrats, computer specialists and combat specialists who are having liberal mindset."

As the truck moved on the gloomy dark road Harbhajan laughed loudly as he drove. Fifty resistance fighters against a mighty empire of military and the powerful Samar Singh! It is a pipe dream!

Chapter 12

Mutant Animals

As the night wore on the shadows deepened and it was charcoal dark all-around. Asha Rao said, "We have to stop somewhere and rest till the morning."

Sathya said "Yeah, there seems to be this village nearby and a group of deserted houses there. Indrani appeared before Asha like a glowing white hologram and said, "I can create a hideout for you. I can use the material in the house. But it is very cold and you must make a fire." "Let's walk" said Doctor Ram "and find a shelter in the outskirts of the village. This village was nearly empty and a few kilometres away from the highway. There was a small house with a garden in the front yard. They were there sitting in the grass while Dheeraj spread bed sheets on the lawns. Indrani said, "I can create something like a shelter. I will search the house." And within half an hour she brought some blankets and mattresses from the house. The blankets and mattresses were laden with dust and ashes but still felt like Heaven for them, with their aching limbs after walking so long on the road. As Asha opened the bags and entered the tent-like shelter, Indrani said, "I will stay on guard for you. Have your dinner with the packed food which was brought from the bunker in the forest."

There were some protein biscuits, but the bread was dried stiff, and jam tasted stale and the lukewarm milk in the thermos was not good, but it was the best food they could have in many days. They all slept in the tent and had a blissful sleep for a few hours only.

There was a gurgling sound coming from behind the house. Dheeraj woke up first. He listened intensively for about a few minutes.

Dheeraj woke up next and said, "What is that?" Doctor Ram slowly got up and listened carefully. As he sat like that the growing increased and there was a wailing of animals in the backyard and surroundings of the house. "Get up! Get up," said Doctor Ram. They are wolves and jackals. Take your guns and be ready. They may attack us anytime!"

The animal suddenly jumped from the back of the house from the shadows on to them. It was a big wolf like animal only bigger than an average wolf. Its eyes were shining red. It had a shining collar of metal around its neck. The fur on its body was scratched in patches as if burnt by fire. It was followed by a pack of smaller wolves and dogs with similar collars around the neck.

"What are these things?" Shouted Asha in terror. "These are the mutant animals which have been modified by radiation. After the explosion they have been programmed and trained by the dictator to attack people and to hunt people who are escaping from the city. Shoot them! You shoot them in the collar around the neck!"

"What's the collar for?" wondered Dheeraj. "You should know better. Because you are the computer specialist. The dictator's regime has put the collar around these animals' neck to control them and to attack and hunt people by remote signals." Meanwhile the wolf suddenly jumped over them. Dr.Ram shouted "Go back, go back! Their bites can be very dangerous. You will get radiation sickness immediately! How do you know? Asked Asha. "I have seen such animal bites, animals attacking people while I was working in the clinic in the village," said Ram. Their shots pierced the body of the animals, but they relentlessly jumped as they ran back into the shadows.

The correct way would be to attack the collars. They are electronically collared to trace their location. Soon some soldiers may come here."

Dheeraj ran after the animal and shot one final time. There was a screeching sound and spark and the wolf fell down wriggling in pain.

"Gotcha." said Ram. "You hit the target."

They could kill a few more ferocious dogs, as they were weak and sick, even though they appeared fearsome outwardly.

"This is all like a nightmare unimaginable," said Asha.

It was past midnight and they had to sleep for a few hours before resuming the journey to the capital.

Dheeraj the computer specialist went outside the house into the courtyard and started talking in whispers on his mobile. "Whom are you talking to?" Asha asked him. "You are having your own secrets!" She came out of the door stealthily and was watching him.

"As if you don't have!" Said derisively Dheeraj. "You are probably the daughter of the Prime Minister, and you never told us."

Sathya said "I knew it all the time. I'm her friend. Why are you worried? Doctor Ram interjected. "Let us not quarrel among ourselves. There is a lot we must do together." Meanwhile Indrani has entered the shelter. She was glowing in dull red colour. "I'm out of charge unfortunately. I am unable to find any charging outlets here. Perhaps for a few hours I will be immobile. I will only use my reserve energy to help you. So, you must look after yourself.". As time passed, they slept and had a sleep full of dreams with wild animals' black shapes and of unknown creatures hissing at them. And when they got up the Sun was shining through the windows, and the sky was clear, and another day had dawned. "Let us start again and not fight among us. We have got a powerful enemy to fight against and an ideal to achieve for." spoke Dr.Ram. "Find whatever is there to eat and let us start. Our old horse, the van, is waiting for us and now we must find the means of charging the Robot.

Dheeraj said. "There may not be any need for charging. It is only a software. Sometimes it enters the brain of Asha sometimes it comes out in the shape of Indrani. That's why Asha is behaving like a Super girl. I am sure the AI is staying in her brain.

Sathya sounded worried. "It's ominous. The soft ware's thinking, and memory could clash with Asha's own memory and individual experiences and decision making, as there is a lot of junk material in her brain, and she may end up with getting headaches and mentally disturbed."

"We will remove the device from her brain once our mission of finding and finishing off the dictator and rescuing her dad is over." said Dheeraj.

"I am already having headaches and multiple images in my brain," cried Asha." But I guess it is a burden I will have to face to save my people and their leader who my dad is, who believes in democracy and equal rights".

"That is a nice speech. But I have nothing but your safety in my mind and will not hesitate to remove it and save you. Very soon." Said Sathya. "Nothing is more precious than you for me."

They quit the tent but soon they were on their way to Delhi. They had hardly any plans to attack or defeat the next creatures or marauders or soldiers which may encounter and attack them.

Except the AI Indrani which now has become a red light shapeless electronic software and was getting charged in Asha's brain.

...And sucking up her energy for want of power.

They could go for some distance in their old, dilapidated truck for about 70 kilometres. It was slow paced. The view from the windows was not pleasant at all. There were trees darkened with acid rain, houses destroyed by fire, and dead animals by the side of the road.

Soon it was noon. The Sun shone palely out of the dark clouds. They found a village on the roadside where they wanted to stop for lunch. "Where is the shade to sit and to take a bite?" wondered Sathya. "You are going poetic." Asha said. "Let us find an empty house!"

There was a rotten metallic smell possibly from the decaying animal cadavers. "We have some bread, and coffee in the thermos let us have our own variety of lunch," said Asha.

They ate slowly without talking much. "We may be in the outskirts of Delhi by dusk." said Dheeraj. "Indrani, can you get access to the map of Delhi? What's happening there now? We must have a plan to enter the city *incognito* and then we must make contact with at least some of the resistance groups. We must have a plan of attacking the General's defence systems. If I am right, he must be having a nuclear cache which is inoperable by him. If we can destroy that system, we can destroy him or fight his forces by guerrilla warfare easily. If I remember well this system of nuclear attack has a self-destruct sequence which is embedded in a code by artificial intelligence. The defence headquarters is somewhere underground on the Delhi Agra highway. Most probably General Samar Singh wants the code to access this system and keep it under his control. Just find the reason why my father had asked me to search for the device which has to be opened by a password." Asha thought as if she was talking aloud. Indrani talked in the tone of a female without any emotion. "The whole Delhi sky is clouded by dark pollution clouds which have been present since the time of the nuclear disaster. I cannot access much of the satellite photographs from the partially operative satellite monitoring systems. But I can tell you that your plans are reasonably logical. When I stayed in your brain, I could access your memories and found that your father has told you about the self-destructing sequence of the nuclear weapons. This system is embedded in a code in a blue tower at the centre of the underground system. If we can break into the underground headquarters, I can access the code with the help of the device and password and destroy the nuclear cache of weapons. It will destroy the General's last hope of control over the remaining country and whatever is left of the world."

"But it may also destroy the city by explosions again," said Sathya.

"Yes. But there is no other way. We must warn the people to evacuate out of the city at least a hundred kilometres out of Delhi."

"But how? "Asked Sathya.

Dr Ram said. "We can utilise the resistance forces. The resistance forces are called the Phoenix forces. There are various secret organisations which are grouping themselves to fight the dictator. We can ask them to help people to travel out of the city."

"And then...? What about us? We will not die?" Asked Dheeraj. "Should we sacrifice ourselves?"

Asha said." May be. May be not. We must have some lag period in which we can escape to a safe bunker or distant place. We must see. My father said that sacrifice is the only way to redemption."

"This is madness." Said Sathya. "I am your boyfriend and madly in love with you. Now you are on a suicidal mission. And I may go down with you. Asha! Don't be silly. Let us escape into the countryside and wait. This is not the way."

"No, my father intended that I fight and save the country. We will organize an escape into a bunker. We will then wear radiation suits and travel to the South where my father may be hiding. Maybe he is alive, and I am sure he must be in a place where his allies are there. One such a place is the city of Hyderabad in the Deccan. It is a hi-tech city with so many Computer -Savy Government and private officials. There are bunkers existing there according to the map in my mind. We will go find him there and..."

And...? asked Sathya. What will we do in the dark aftermath of nuclear winter where no agriculture exists, no food and no people to work?

"We will reconstruct. We will find ways to raise again. We will take the help of AI. Like a phoenix we will rise again." As she talked her voice was half human and half robotic. "You can stay with me, or you can leave. That's your call. Sathya! I love you. But I love the country and our freedom more. Make your decision." She turned towards Dr Ram and Dheeraj as the AI Indrani hovered around as a hologram of bright light.

"Doctor and Dheeraj, this is for you too. Though I need you, I won't insist that you join me in this perilous mission. I have Indrani designed by my father's intelligence. I will go alone. You can find your own ways."

There was silence for a long time. A vulture fluttered its wings somewhere on a dried branch of a tree. Suddenly there was a draught of air with odour of dying animals. It was desolate with the suddenly darkening radiation clouds.

"We will be with you. There is no doubt. "Said Sathya I will live or die with you only. To hell with it, this is the apocalypse. What else is the option? What will I do without you?"

"We too…" said Dheeraj "and its destiny which united us. And we will do whatever we can."

Indrani the AI could not laugh. She had a mechanical voice. "Now it is settled. Let us move. It may rain acid any time now."

"Like phoenix we will rise. Asha said. "We will contact the other phoenix forces and attack soon."

They ran towards the truck covering their eyes as the first drops of rain started falling.

Chapter 13

Desolate City

Six months after the devastating nuclear attack on Delhi, the once bustling city now was lying in ruins. The air, thick with ash and sorrow, hung heavily over the desolate streets. The glimpse of the aftermath was not heartening at all.

The streets were empty. The roads, once teeming with life, were eerily empty. Buildings stood as hollow shells, their windows shattered, and walls scorched. Nature had begun to reclaim the concrete jungle, with weeds pushing through the cracks in the pavement. The clouds were ashen. The sky, perpetually grey, bore witness to the recent catastrophe. Sunsets were a haunting blend of crimson and ash, casting long shadows over the remnants of civilization. The air smelt of burnt wood and despair. There were few survivors. Those few resilient souls wandered the streets, their faces masked to protect against lingering radiation. Children, orphaned by the cataclysm, clutched makeshift toys, a stark contrast to the horrors they've witnessed. One could witness makeshift shelters at sporadic places. Families huddled in such makeshift shelters, like, abandoned metro stations, half -collapsed buildings, and underground bunkers. They shared meagre rations and stories of lost loved ones. Then there was the drip. The famous monuments like Taj Mahal and other offices stood as grim reminders of lost grandeur. Their once-gleaming surfaces now bore the scars from the blast. And yet there were whispers of hope. Amid despair, whispers of hope circulated. Rumours of a secret underground network, the Phoenix Collective spread. They allegedly provided aid, information, and glimpses of a better future. In the silence of these broken streets, one truth remained: humanity always endures, even in the darkest of times. In such a gloomy aftermath of the nuclear apocalypse, Asha Rao, daughter of the exiled Prime Minister Vikram Rao, embarked on a perilous mission, one that would alter the course of history and bring hope to the remnants of humanity.

Chapter 14

The *Dhaba*

As they entered the city it was past 8 pm. They parked the vehicle in a suburb where it would be inconspicuous among the other dilapidated trucks in the old truck bay and walked with their bags and masks in radiation suits. Soon they found a roadside thatched hut or *dhaba* with a few people in turbans sitting inside. "It's lucky that we found a *dhaba* at this time." exclaimed Dheeraj. They went inside and found a haggard old man in front of a stainless-steel box apparently containing preserved food like rotis and a steel flask which hopefully might be having some tea. "*Bhaiya*! please give two *rotis* each for us. We are coming from a long way. And one cup of chai for everyone. How much it would cost?" asked Asha.

"The times are bad *memsab*. It would cost you 2000 rupees in hard currency only. It is very difficult to get by in Delhi these days after the bomb." grumbled the old man.

"Where can we get cash Baba!" Asha said in despair. "For everything there is only cash to be paid. Everything is costly. You must know it is the bomb which we had on our heads. I bring these items at a premium from the black market. With that money I have to look after my own family. There are no supplies anymore in the city. It is a big black famine, memsaab."

"We had been living for months in the wild after the explosion. We were eating and scavenging rotten stuff and we had come to Delhi to join the forces which fight the General, and you refuse to give us food."

Asha took her gold chain from her neck and gave it to him. The old man's eyes widened in surprise. It is too valuable *memsab*. He looked again at her face and shouted in surprise. At once he burst into Hindi. You are the daughter of the Prime Minister Rao, aren't you? I have seen you many a time on the TV. *Amma*, you are like my daughter. Your friends are like my sons. Take all this and eat all you want. I am with you in the fight against Singh. We heard rumours that you are coming back and joining the phoenix forces from a long time. But it was never to be. Now you are here at last."

"First give us the food. We eat and then talk what is this phoenix about." said Dheeraj.

As the old man served them *rotis* and some potato curry which tasted not very bad considering the circumstances they regained their strength and drank the water from the earthen pots in the *dhaba*.

"Now tell me what has been happening in this city after the explosion. Is not General Samar Singh looking after the poor? I heard the last city has been almost completed."

"Yes. But at what cost? Many people died while constructing the underground city. Many more people died in the famine. Many more people died without being paid proper wages and starved to death. Meanwhile the General did not care and went on building the city. The few remaining people obeyed him taking the meagre wages or whatever crumbs of bread or currency he was giving. Many fled from the city and escaped to the countryside. But what is the use? There are no fields growing food grains anymore, there are no shops selling food except through black market with the material which has come from the rich people's houses and through smuggling across the border from neighbouring countries. We few people who are old and helpless are existing like this."

They listened silently.

As they finished and gulped the *lassi* which was a little stale in taste, Asha asked slowly almost in a whisper.

"Baba... please tell me what is this phoenix group about? Do you know any contacts?"

There was a perceptible change in the expression of the old man.

Fear and apprehension showed clearly in his flicker of eyelids and quivering of lips.

"I don't know anything. I do small business and anyways who are you and how can you save me if I get killed by the troops? Leave me alone. Eat your food and leave as you paid good money. *Chalé jao!*"

"OK Baba. We will not bother you with difficult questions. They ate and finished the food silently and walked out of the dilapidated *dhaba* which posed as a restaurant for the needy in the difficult times.

"Indrani! Can you help me by hacking and hearing the communication systems which are partially existing in the city of New Delhi? How to find out encrypted messages exchanging among these groups?" Asha asked looking at Indrani who just appeared as a hologram by her side.

"Definitely I can. Encrypted messages are only the way how they can communicate with each other. I will hack into the partially existing secret encrypted system and we would search for the word phoenix. Let us settle down in a place where we are not found."

It was getting darker, and the roads fell silent and as they walked on the street, they found a partially destroyed Supermarket housed in broken walls and a lot of debris. They went into the inner hall full of burnt-out shelves still having charred food crumbs and groceries. They found a few plastic chairs at the end of a glass wall and sat there. Indrani in her translucent holographic form stood and conjured the holographic map which showed messages under the heading of the Google renaissance net. This was obviously restored after the nuclear Holocaust. It existed in various places in some form or other. One would think that the Internet headquarters was in the United States somewhere hidden and was built resistant to even nuclear attacks. All the transponders the satellites and others server systems were destroyed but still some partial networks existed. There were several dots in gibberish alphabets conversing with each other on the screen which was transparent enough to show the other side of the racks also. After half an hour off silently searching Indrani said "Woohoo…I found it. I could decrypt the cipher code. Every step after 3 lines I find a diagram of a bird rising from ash. "Oh!" said Dheeraj." I do make it out. It is the phoenix bird which is the symbol of the phoenix collective. It must be."

Indrani said mechanically. "You are right Dheeraj Master. It is the phoenix collective which is communicating with each other. By plotting their conversations, I can make out that there are at least three underground secret quarters and latitudes, from where they are coming. What do the conversations are about?" asked Dheeraj.

"Mostly nothing important. Except, how are you, have you taken food, let us go for a drink, how is the weather? … etcetera. But I can make out that there is a code in their conversations and the most important thing for me is that I can make out the places where they are hiding in. That can be important for you."

And so it went on into the middle of the night. At last Dheeraj could make out their latitudes and longitudes which should be underground somewhere under the Red Fort and its surrounding ruins. Sathya said. "Let us sleep at least for now. Tomorrow we will search for their hiding. Asha, you must take care of your health. Indrani, you too can deactivate yourself for the time being. Indrani said, "I will deactivate myself only when Asha gives me a command. "Okay" said Asha. "Deactivate until 6:00 o'clock in the morning and wake up at that time! Doctor Ram said. "Search any sofas here to lie down. Maybe I could give you all some sleeping pills so that you can rest. You have worked too hard."

Then they all slept blissfully as the night wore on silently.

Chapter 15

Viplav

Viplav! Viplav! the man in the olive-green uniform with his face fully covered except for the eyes, was trying to wake him up.

The place was dark and under the ground with solid brick walls and a few vents left for the surface supply of oxygen. Viplav was in a reverie. He was leading the final assault on Samar Singh's underground palace. He had Samar Singh bound in chains and got all his cabinet ministers captured.

"The people's court sentences you to death by firing squad for all the treason and crimes against humanity you committed for your selfish ends" He was reading the judgement.

Then something happened…some robotic soldiers appeared from nowhere and were firing laser guns. The bullets hit Viplav in the chest and legs, and he screamed in excruciating pain. He could see all his comrades in arms in the revolution collapsing in slow motion.

He woke up with a start. It took him and the man waking him up a while to realise that it was all a bad dream. Yes, it could never happen. The scarcely armed feeble Phoenix collective could never capture the powerful dictator backed up with army, lot of technology, money and the rich business supporting him. It was also rumoured that Singh had a cache of nuclear arms which again could be used on his enemies. He had access to the most well-furnished underground bunkers well furnished with food water and power supply which could last for month. How to defeat such a powerful General?

As he was slowly coming to his senses Rohini, a tall girl came into the bunker. She was rather unusually tall with dark black hair in a red shirt and black pants. "Comrade Viplav,"she talked in a tone with anxiety and apprehension. "We have been tracked by some unknown but friendly people."

"What is it now Rohini? If they are friendly what is the worry? Who are they anyway?"

They have given a message to our IP address that they are people from Asha Rao the daughter of Prime Minister Vikram Rao who fled the city. She identified herself as Indrani and asked to communicate with them. She said they would like to join the fight against General Samar Singh, and she is with them. She wanted a place of *rendezvous* to meet one of our representatives on how to plan an offensive. Viplav got up in excitement. "It's a wonderful news. Rumour has it that Asha Rao has access to top secret codes which can hack the army defence system as she was a technology minister in the previous government. With Vikram Rao dead or underground somewhere Asha Rao can lead us, and we will have a strategy to attack. Give her a point somewhere in the city to meet me this evening itself at 6:00 PM. OK? May God help the revolution!

"Yes, comrade. God certainly helped the revolution."

The bunker was cool and calm with some sparse food material and earthen pots filled with cool water. There was a table in the corner with kettle and a few cups with tea powder and milk to make tea. Viplav went and made himself a teacup which was cold but still rejuvenating in the circumstances. They found this bunker which was apparently abandoned by the owners for want of proper and insufficient water supply. There were such abandoned bunkers scattered around the underground in Delhi, while in another corner the last city was being built with fully furnished underground bunkers and some surface buildings supplied with power water and food supply from imports and surrounding villages. Viplav thought, if Asha Rao knows the codes to break into the nuclear cache of the General which is very much possible as she had access to the codes during her tenure as a minister for technology, a plan can be made how to attack the General with his own arms. That is the only way to replace the Government which is killing the people and was bent on acquiring money for itself and was never asking for aid or help from any other international countries. General Samar Singh became greedy. As there were no communications and contact with the outside world, he utilised the people only to construct his city along with his rich coterie of friends who helped him with funds. It was not clear whether he had that technology or even if a plan to save are rebuild the country and help the poor people. They must destroy his arms and army and eliminate him physically. Only then it would be possible to reconstruct a nuclear ravaged India and help all the suffering people all over the scattered surviving communities. As he sipped the cold tea on his table and ate the stale bread with 3 days old jam Viplav consoled himself. "God helps those who help themselves. But do I believe in God, I being an atheist? But still in these circumstances it is always better to pray to a God or any superpower to help. And help is coming really from the most unforeseen quarters but the most possible person who could only deliver the people from certain destruction soon. Rohini came again and spoke. "Good news chief. I told them the time of the appointment and they agreed. They have given passwords. We must tell those passwords on meeting, and we should not carry any arms with us and only two persons, a leader and an assistant must come. That is their advice. and a condition possibly."

"Fair enough!" said Viplav. I will do that. I am eager to meet the daughter of the good Prime Minister after all. She is the only star and hope for us at this point. A few more persons in red uniforms and berets came into the room. They had guns in their hands and their eyes were shining with the bright light of alertness that had come with the long months of underground fighting.

"Let's prepare ourselves, soldiers of the Phoenix! Cheer up! Once we meet the friendly group of Prime minister's daughter, we will inform all other Phoenix collective group around the country to prepare themselves for the final battle."

"Yes commander! Long live the revolution of the Phoenix!" all of them shouted in their shrill voices mixed with hope and excitement.

Chapter 16

Samar Singh

General Samar Singh looked at his image in the mirror with a golden frame in front of him and twisted the grey and white moustache with his little finger up and grunted.

Ah! Now that I found Vikram's daughter, it is only a question of time when I will catch her and retrieve the code for the remaining bombs. Then I can rule the whole damaged country without anyone fighting back. Even the neighbouring countries will not dare threaten me."

For a bunker it was very spacious. General Samar Singh had his headquarters in this place since he occupied the seat of power in Delhi. He had access to all the control systems here like communications CCTV monitoring and switch panel for launching drones which would transmit images of the countryside.

There was a small tapping sound, and a lady entered the bunker from inside room. She was about fifty-five and had dressed herself in dark blue saree covering her head and the diamond rings from her ears shown brilliantly in the grey shadows of the bunker as it was illuminated only by the wall panelling.

"You are talking to yourself? Said she in a mocking tone. "Are you happy that you found Asha Rao? And how? Explain!"

"We had found her in our routine surveillance by the drone cameras. We have been also surveying the movements of the phoenix groups. Both the party of Asha Rao and the phoenix group were found by our surveillance cameras. I am deliberately waiting and arranged a crack team of rapid commandos to catch them at their point of secret meeting."

"How many people would you kill before you look after the welfare of the people?" she asked seriously now.

"I am not going to kill them, especially Asha Rao. The phoenix group itself is expendable. But not Asha. I need her alive to break the code or give the device containing the code to open the last cache of nuclear bombs hidden in our defence headquarters. As it is, we are the only power in the world who are left with some nuclear bombs. I can negotiate with other countries threatening them with counter attacks and get some food and aid for our people. Don't you think it is a good idea? If the erstwhile PM's daughter helps me, I can even give her an important post in the Government so that the people will cooperate with me."

Kalindi, for that was the name of the woman who was talking and was the wife of General Samar Singh just laughed loudly.

"Do you really think that Asha Rao will help you, you who is responsible for the destruction of this country and removal of Prime Minister Vikram Rao? And there is no love lost between you and the people of Delhi or even for that matter in other parts of the destroyed country. You are ruling with an iron fist and there are problems of food supply, anarchy and revolution in the countryside." She gasped in a sigh of desperation.

"Stop it!" shouted the General. "As if it is not enough for me to have opposition outside, there is a critical opposition minister in my own house! Thank you, but no talking any more. Please leave me to my own work."

"That is exactly what I came for. The Defence minister, the minister of intelligence and some other officers have come into the conference room. It seems a meeting is scheduled in 10 minutes. You may go! Please stop your speeches of self-aggrandizement before the mirror. Sometimes I feel that you are going nuts with all your megalomania!"

"It's not megalomania my dear writer wife! I must appear tough and decisive before them. So, I practice. That's all. After all I realise only too well that we are in a hopeless situation!" "But then it's you who started all this by your greed to grab power and started the holocaust!"

"No honey, it is not me who pushed the button of nuclear missiles. I did march to the capital with my loyal rebel troops to remove Vikram from power. I agree. But sensing my plan, it's Vikram who pushed the button of nuclear arms and generated a chain reaction. I do not know why he panicked and harmed the entire world. Still, some of my aides tell me that it was not his intention. He pushed only a false alarm button but somehow the system started a nuclear war of mad destruction. It is all the fault of the latest Artificial Intelligence systems. They were never really evaluated properly by even the most developed countries and were installed as a deterrent only. But still, it is the sin of Vikram. He should have surrendered to me. For this crime I will have to kill him and his daughter. People still think that it's me who is responsible! I will not accept that!"

Kalindi sighed. "Each political one has his own justification. The people suffer as always. I will not stop you. Go ahead. But I only want to see the Sun rise again in a clear sky, the green trees and love to have pure air. Just the normal Earth like before. You both did this crime of destruction, and humanity suffers."

General Samar Singh grunted and spoke.

"I will have to rule and ultimately the power is mine. I can rule the world with the remaining nuclear cache if I only I know the way. Do not come in the way of my ambition which had come true but in a perverted way."

"Have your tea before you go to the meeting. She pointed to the table where white porcelain teacups and kettles with steaming water tea powder and milk were served and ready.

"Thanks for at least now playing the wife!"

"Good luck dear. These are bad times and worse should not happen."

Kalindi was a poetess and nature lover and peaceful housewife though she was with the tough military man as lover and wife since his student days and his growth in the armed forces.

"Oh! For a simple thing like normal air and a red rose with fragrance and blue sky with white clouds…"

"I pine for olden days of *Holi* and *Dussehra* and fairs and pilgrimages in the open air and a red Sunset with the blue Moon raising once in a while and pigeons fluttering in the silence! I hate this bunker life!"

Chapter 17

Phoenix

It was past midnight and the shadowy figures waited for the big cargo truck which had to take them to the secret meeting point.

Viplav and his close lieutenant clad in dark shirts and pants with faces covered with woollen shawls to beat the cold and also to be *incognito*.

"Harbhajan should come any moment now. He knows all places and routes in Delhi like the palm of his hand" Said Viplav.

In a few minutes the dark truck came with dimmed lights and stopped in front of them. Anyone would think it was a transport lorry coming into Chandini Chowk to drop some packages.

Harbhajan was in the driving seat and waved with his hand to ask them to get in.

Soon the lorry moved to the Agra road for the rendezvous with Asha Rao and her group. It was important not to be caught by the occasional patrol police or by the drone cameras.

Samar Singh had a good surveillance system and was always checking for renegades as well as the PM's daughter and her group.

In the present world global positioning systems and mobile mapping systems were not functioning. They had to follow the instructions to the place given by the team of Asha Rao and Harbhajan was a capable driver. He was now with the resistance, having lost track of all his family and he was being hunted by the army for killing a few guards and running away from work.

As they approached the partly destroyed building which was once a supermarket called *"Lakshmi Bazaar"*, they heard a distant sound.

"Oh! This could be a night police patrol!" Said the aide of Viplav.

"Be cool. We have our identity cards and can explain."

In a few minutes the head lights of a police vehicle beamed high in front of their truck. As Harbhajan slowly stopped, the loudspeaker mounted on the police patrol vehicle shouted.

"Stop! Identify yourselves! The driver please come out! It was the hoarse voice of the patrol police. Harbhajan slowly got down from the vehicle and stood on the road. Viplav and his aide clutched their guns. The air was still with tension. Viplav clearly was aware that his photo was on every policeman's list as the most wanted resistance fighter. A patrol policeman got down from his vehicle with a big torchlight and focused on the identity documents of Harbhajan. "Who are the others in the vehicle?" he asked and "What is the cargo you are carrying?"

Harbhajan did have a duplicate identity card with the name of Harish David and to suit this name he has already shaved his beard moustache and sported a golf cap to complete the picture of a Christian identity. "Saab, this is a garbage transport vehicle we are carrying the night garbage and night soil from the slum areas to the dumping yard outside the city." It was past 1:00 o'clock after the midnight and the patrol man did not want to sniff around the foul-smelling garbage. He had to eat his dinner yet. "They are your helpers in the driving cabin?"

"Yes! Sir! We have to go a long way and empty all the load. So, I took two persons along with me. This awful work can only be done in the night time." *Theek hai chalo*" the policeman departed in his vehicle as the tension lightened in the driver's cabin with the loosening of the grip on the guns. Harbhajan came back and drove the vehicle ahead. Soon they found two blinking lights in the *Lakshmi Bazaar* and all the three got down and entered the building. Soon the meeting with the team of Asha Rao with Viplav started. It was an emotional reunion and the most important event in the post nuclear scenario of the country. They exchanged details of the suffering and travails of the people and the cruelty of the dictator and his police. Everybody had a story.

Soon somebody served hot sizzling tea this time, which freshened them up, and then Asha Rao said, "The past is past, now let us think of an attack and removal of the dictator Samar Singh. I have to fulfil my personal vendetta as well as the cause of the people."

"Let us have a plan of attack on the underground bunkers where Samar Singh stays and directs the military. We have some maps. You can chalk out a plan with the help of AI who is with you "

"You know that I have AI?"

"Yes. Madam. We do know that her name is Indra…and you have access codes to defence systems of this dictator."

"You have some really good information and please you can call me Asha and not Madam. And this woman is the AI in woman shape of hologram. And slight correction, her name is Indrani. You give the maps and coordinates to her, and she will give us a picture."

Indrani stepped out of the shadows. A blue glow emanated from her in front of her face showing the map of Delhi which gradually narrowed down to the building with their sign board written Security Headquarters. I have retrieved it from my memory system. This is the headquarters both on the surface as well as on the underground of General Samar Singh. The underground headquarters contains the defence system with missiles stored in silos targeted towards neighbouring countries as well as our own country. But the general has no access to the password with Asha Rao being the only one having access to the system. She has it in her device. She can enter the headquarters with her handprint and only she can enter it. But there is a three layered defence system around the headquarters which is guarded by rapid action forces with rocket launchers and missiles. To access the system, we must either defeat the 3 layers of defence and enter the underground or go there in disguise which is not possible. The plan would be your resistance forces must attack the surrounding forces of Samar Singh first and then Asha Rao along with me and her group can enter the underground headquarters and disable the systems. The systems can be either disabled or a self-destruct sequence can be initiated. The last card of Samar Singh is to threaten the remaining country and their surrounding countries with his remaining nuclear systems so that he can control them. If we can destroy this or deactivate this, Samar Singh will be easily defeated. He can be captured and executed so we want your soldiers and the resistance fighters to attack at a particular date and disable the surrounding security layer and give us a signal. Then Asha, myself with my artificial intelligence mapping and Dheeraj with his computer expertise can enter the underground. Asha would deactivate or change the code of the system to initiate a self-destruct sequence which will cause an implosion. Doctor Ram will help us in any medical emergency and Sathya as he is a pilot will wait outside at a particular spot with a helicopter which has to be stolen from the forces and to keep for us as a getaway vehicle because the fire following the explosion definitely will be severe and the surroundings will be in flames up to 3 kilometres at least. So you have to decide a date and time for this plan. We need the phoenix resistance forces to disable the surrounding forces." It was an exhaustive discussion and the discussions and plans went on late into the night and all of them hatched out a plan within three days. The AI Indrani took the numbers of contact and finalized the plan by exact timings.

"We must communicate by whatever existing mobile systems or walkie talkies. The plan will be called "Operation Freedom" It will start 3 days after midnight at 1:00 AM exactly. The phoenix soldiers must attack in their vehicles with weapons and destroy the three layers of security."

And then they had some hot coffee and biscuits and left the place with a final determination to defeat the dictator.

Indrani the AI in the shape of hologram sometimes manifested outside and sometimes went into the brain of Asha as a software system to access her thoughts through the device in her brain. It was something extraordinary and caused headache and vertigo and hallucinations to Asha, but she had by now learnt to live with it. It was the part of the emergency plan created by Vikram Rao the PM. For Asha was Indrani. Indrani was Asha, her *alter ego.*

Chapter 18

Cabinet Meeting

The Cabinet meeting was brief but not without its fireworks. General Samar Singh addressed the ministers and the top defence personnel in a fierce speech.

"Dear friends and officers, the time of reckoning has come. We are coming through to rehabilitate the country after the nuclear Holocaust which was accidental and deliberate mistake of the previous Prime Minister. We have been destroyed completely and the world has been destroyed mostly. We are trying to conserve our resources and rebuild the city. In this process we had to do a lot of tough actions and make the people work hard with an iron hand stop because that is the only way to come out of this situation. Now the phoenix resistance groups are doing sabotage and the latest is we have information that the erstwhile prime minister's daughter Asha Rao has entered the city and is planning an attack on our installations. Add this is ominous because she, being the daughter of that ex-Prime Minister has access to all the secret codes of the remaining installations in the underground headquarters which exists under my residence. This nuclear cache is important because it is one of the few remaining nuclear arms in the world and if I can unleash it I can control the whole world with it by threatening to explode it but I do not have access to this woman whom we believe has access to this and is planning to attack us with her rebel resistance groups called phoenix. They are renegades and outlaws and are determined to plunder the Government's wealth and take it away in the name of distribution to the poor. We are planning an operation to prevent them and we are attacking them preemptively. I need your support for this action which could be the end of all of our suffering Another war would cause more damage too."

He went on like this but did not explain his plan. The Defence minister rose up and talked loudly. "Your excellency! Will you please listen to me once? The General's face switched in expression of anger, but he said "Go on"

"I think it would be a futile exercise to fight among ourselves and to kill our own people. We are sure that Asha Rao can open the nuclear arms and it can cause a lot of damage for everybody and the constructions whatever we have made for the last city in Delhi would be destroyed if there is an explosion which could be triggered by Asha Rao's knowledge of the codes as she was the minister for technology. We had enough of nuclear wars and destruction and the people are suffering. I suggest we negotiate with these rebels and Asha Rao and start a new Government which is representative of the people's wishes and go on with our reconstruction in these dire times." There was cacophony in the cabinet room with some people supporting this and some people against it. General Samar Singh said finally almost in a shouting way in his garrulous tone. "Gentlemen! I know what is best for the country. These people must be stopped. Unless they are stopped and the nuclear arms are in my hands, I cannot control the vast resources of this country and I cannot make others help us."

"This is madness!" said the Defence Minister and the Minister for Finance. The others said, "Yes! We support the General." Finally General Samar Singh said "I close the meeting. My decision is final. Now the cabinet members left in disgust and in in silence as they knew very well that they could be killed for insubordination by the cruel General. And also, none of them had any clue of what was the action the General was going to take against the rebel forces.

"Please confine yourself to the underground bunkers while I fight them. That's an order and you must obey the orders. These are dire times." said the General and their meeting ended.

As the meeting ended, and the officials departed for their bunker homes sirens already sounded like the hooting of owls to suggest an emergency and to alert the armed forces. Most of the ministers lived in underground bunkers made in the centre of the city which was once the Central Vista. Major buildings like the parliament and Rashtrapati Bhavan were standing intact even though with charred blackened walls. They were uninhabited and empty now. For, most of the Government shifted to the underground bunkers. The President himself was not there and was believed to have been killed or in exile after the nuclear bombs struck.

The soldiers lived in the cantonment on the surface in radiation suits and masks and they were to be always ready for fighting on call. Some soldiers did have radiation sickness and died periodically. A few important officers only stayed underground to give them orders. There were no fighter planes worth their name. There were no monitoring cells or operating Headquarters. There were no planes. Of course there were a few armed trucks and tanks which were intact after the war. The way one made war had completely changed after the Holocaust. Breaking the silence some of the soldiers with guns came out of the bunkers in their radiation suits. A few had oxygen masks and some mounted in the jeeps. One or two tanks moved as if to guard the Central Vista of the administrative underground quarters. The sky was dark and grey as the dusk fell and a long night descended on the silent capital. The interminable wait began for the attack which could come anytime from the resistance forces, but they did not know how or when.

Chapter 19

Strategy

The strategic planning to attack went on for three hours with discussions among the group with Asha Rao and Indrani giving the final nod for every step.

There are three layers of defence for the General's headquarters, home as well as the remaining cache of nuclear missile systems which are located underground.

Viplav and his group of resistance will attack with guns the outer defence which had two turrets each side of the big gate and soldiers guarding the ten feet wall surrounding the entrance to the underground. The second layer was the entrance to the underground with a door guarded by a pass key possibly a hand print or code word. It led to steps into the underground tunnels which led to the final bunkers having the office, home and Headquarters of military with silos of nuclear missiles of the General.

They were his trump card to threaten the opposition in the country and bargain with other countries in the world.

"But only you, Asha, have the device to open the missile system," said Sathya.

Viplav and his army will attack the outer first layer of the defence wall at midnight. Then we move in.

Sathya will wait with a helicopter as a getaway vehicle.

Dheeraj will help to hack the computer systems.

Dr.Ram will accompany us and give medicines or …"

"I can use tranquilizer guns to deactivate some soldiers or General Samar Singh without killing him," said Dr Ram.

"Fine. Let us get ready but first Indrani and Sathya have to procure a helicopter for us." Said Asha.

"Sure. How to steal a helicopter?" Sathya quizzed.

"Not one but two. One as a getaway vehicle and another to cover Viplav after he attacks the first layer of defence."

"I can hack into the defence systems and places of helicopter hangars and give you the map and locations." Said Indrani.

"OK. Then we will put one as a getaway vehicle and one for attack. For this I have to bring in two helicopters ha, ha!" Sathya said.

"You have to do your own planning and execution with Indrani. And your time to prove yourselves has come now."

As they discussed this Indrani the AI had announced, "Watch this!"

It was an announcement of General Samar Singh on the local TV and the existing networks.

"Dear countrymen! The irresponsible phoenix rebels are going to attack my Government which is doing the unenviable task of running the Government in the difficult post nuclear situation. I am still having some arms and missiles with me and I can use them at will if these renegades want to spoil my efforts of rebuilding the country. The neighbouring countries! Beware of me if you cannot give aid or food to Delhi, I can unleash the arms on you again and throw you into more turmoil. Not only that there is more. I can release the mutants and hungry animals changed dangerously by radiation on the world only to make it a more chaotic waste land…"

His speech went on like that and anyone with some common sense could make out that he was under pressure or turned into a psychopath. Or he was planning to threaten them with some ulterior motive.

"It is obvious that he has no key to use those weapons. Because the device given by my father is with me. This is only an empty threat." said Asha.

Indrani the AI woman said, "Yes his tone suggests megalomania and a lack of judgement. Or he is aware we are hearing him and challenging us to come."

"We definitely will, then. We will disarm the missile system, imprison or kill the dictator and bring back the rule of democracy and rebuild the country. The poor suffered more and are still suffering and we have to save them." said Asha with determination. She was a leader now.

"We are with you!" all of them echoed as the shadows of the long night were slowly disappearing with the pale Sun rising behind the dark clouds.

Chapter 20

Helicopter

Sathya checked his VR glasses, making sure they were connected to Indrani, the AI that was guiding him and Harbhajan through the ruins of Delhi. He could see a map of the city, with red dots indicating the locations of General Samar Singh's patrols and checkpoints. He could also see a green dot, marking the helicopter base that was their target.

"Indrani, are you there?" he whispered into his earpiece.

"Yes, I'm here. I'm monitoring the situation and updating the map in real time. You're about two kilometres away from the base. There's a patrol coming your way. Hide behind the rubble and wait for them to pass," Indrani said in a calm voice.

Sathya nodded and signalled to Harbhajan, who was driving the truck that they had stolen from a supply convoy. They pulled over and got out of the truck, hiding behind a pile of concrete and metal that used to be a skyscraper. They watched as a jeep with four soldiers drove by, oblivious to their presence.

"Okay, they're gone. You can move now. Follow the route that I've marked for you. It's the safest and fastest way to the base. Avoid the main roads and the bridges. They're heavily guarded and mined," Indrani said.Sathya and Harbhajan got back into the truck and followed Indrani's instructions. They drove through the narrow streets and alleys, dodging the debris and the corpses that littered the ground. They could see the signs of the nuclear war that had devastated the city and the country. Buildings collapsed, cars were burnt, trees were charred, and the sky was dark with smoke.

They reached the outskirts of the base, which was surrounded by a high wall and a barbed wire fence. There was a gate with a guard post, but Indrani had hacked into the security system and opened it for them. "Good job, Indrani. You are a genius," Sathya said.

"Thank you, Sathya. But do not celebrate yet. You still have to get inside the base and steal a helicopter. And you must do it fast. The General is planning to launch a missile attack on Hyderabad in an hour. You must stop him," Indrani said.

"I know, I know. Do not worry, we will do it. Harbhajan, are you ready?" Sathya asked. "Ready as ever, brother. Let us do this," Harbhajan said. They drove into the base, pretending to be part of the General's forces. They wore the uniforms and the badges that they had taken from the soldiers they had killed. They also had fake papers and IDs that Indrani had forged for them.

They parked the truck near a hangar, where several helicopters were parked. They got out of the truck and walked towards the hangar, acting casual and confident. "Hey, you there! Stop! Where are you going?" a voice shouted behind them. They turned and saw a sergeant with a rifle pointing at them. He had a suspicious look on his face.

"We're here to deliver some supplies for the helicopters. We have the orders from the General himself," Sathya said, showing him the fake papers. The sergeant looked at the papers and frowned. "These papers are fake. You're not from the General's forces. You're spies. You're traitors. You're dead," he said, raising his rifle. Sathya and Harbhajan reacted quickly. They drew their pistols and shot the sergeant in the head. He fell to the ground, blood spilling from his wound.

"Damn it. We've been compromised. Indrani, we need a diversion. Now," Sathya said.

"I'm on it. I've set off the alarms and the sprinklers in the other hangars. That should distract the guards and the pilots. Hurry up and get to the helicopter. I've already unlocked the one that's closest to you. It's a Black Hawk. It has enough fuel and ammo to get you to Hyderabad and back. Go, go, go," Indrani said.

Sathya and Harbhajan ran to the helicopter, ignoring the sirens and the shouts that filled the air. They got inside the cockpit and strapped themselves in. Sathya took the controls and started the engine. The blades began to spin, creating a loud noise.

"Indrani, we're in. How do we get out of here?" Sathya asked.

"Follow my directions. I've cleared a path for you. There's a gap in the wall on the east side of the base. Fly through it and head south. You'll reach the Defence Headquarters in thirty minutes. Good luck, Sathya. Good luck, Harbhajan. You're the only hope for this country. You're the only hope for this world," Indrani said. "Thank you, Indrani. You're the best. We'll see you soon. Over and out," Sathya said.

He lifted the helicopter off the ground and flew towards the gap in the wall. He saw a few soldiers shooting at them, but he ignored them. He flew through the gap and out of the base. He looked at the horizon and saw the sun rising over the ruins of Delhi. He smiled and said to Harbhajan, "We did it, brother. We did it. We stole a helicopter. Now let's go and help Asha in the final attack. Let's go and save the world. Harbhajan smiled back and said, "Let's go, brother. Let's go."

"We have to procure one more helicopter again for our plan" said Sathya. "Of course, we will come back again. We got this. Said Harbhajan. He was laughing loudly after a long time.AI Indrani settled in the back of the chopper and said in its mechanical voice. "It may not be easy but this time we will hijack one. I will tell you how."

Chapter 21

The Attack

The attack on the first layer of defence started about 1:00 AM by Viplav and his phoenix resistance forces. The outer layer was about seven kilometres from the main underground bunker of General Samar Singh. It had an iron fencing with towers guarded by soldiers, but they had no inkling of any imminent attack. It was obvious that Viplav and his associates had an easy win over them, till the soldiers in the second line of defence which was about three kilometres from the headquarters were alerted by both drone cameras and the alarm systems. They quickly responded with helicopter guns and bombs which were fired from above on the advancing resistance troops.

There was a lot of fire and smoke, screams and death. Phoenix fighters of the resistance were like wild ducks in the open for the helicopter guns which were showering bullets on them from above meanwhile dozens of soldiers of Samar Singh showered laser bullets on them in front. The battle went on for about two hours till dawn with a lot of casualties on each side.

But Viplav somehow survived and started his attack on the second line of defence which was a concrete wall ten feet high backed by soldiers with field guns on tanks. Viplav was ferocious in fighting. His assistants were not caring for their lives and many died with only a few people surviving. And finally they broke the barrier with a hand held bomb directly exploding the headquarters of this second line of defence. Indrani the AI was tracking all the information from the drone cameras by hacking into the communications of Samar Singh. Dheeraj who also had hacked into the systems said. "It is all unbelievably bad. Viplav is dying and he is like a sitting duck in front of them."

Asha Rao was watching in her night glasses. Doctor Ram said in a worried tone "My need is there. I had to treat them. There are many wounded and suffering in pain. "That is a noble gesture from you Doc.But obviously you cannot go there at this time of firing. Let us wait," said Asha Rao. As the sun rose in the East a red light descended on the scene of the battle where the bodies were stretched helter- skelter on the ground and bleeding soldiers groaned endlessly. And smoke from the guns and the bombs was enveloping the air. Asha said "It is time now for us to go and break open the underground bunker. We have to go in our helicopter and enter the underground headquarters as quickly as possible."

Meanwhile deep in the underground bunker General Samar Singh was holding a meeting with his closest aides and was monitoring the surveillance cameras which were transmitting information on the various screens in front of him. The chiefs of the defence staff who were about three in number and were closest confidants to him wore a worried look and one said "General this is unexpected. The phoenix forces could never have got this far without the help of Asha Rao or without the encouragement or coercion by her. At the best they were small-time resistance forces attacking markets, stealing supplies like clothes and food and helping the slum area people. They could never have ventured to attack directly the Government Headquarters. This could be a serious problem for us."

General Samar Singh said grimly. "Only Asha Rao has the code for starting or destroying the weapon system which is remaining with me. It is my plan to attract her to this place so that I can have access to the nuclear arms. As soon as she comes, I can kill her and open the nuclear arms, and can use them to bargain for my position in the world and in the country. Once I have the nuclear arms which I can use on anybody the smaller warlords and the foreign powers will listen to me with fear and respect. This is the only way for us to survive. Let her come, let me see, let me take my chances. One she comes searching for the last remaining nuclear cache of arms I am going to trap her and kill her. You just wait in the shadows around the hall of mirrors inside which is holding the missile system." No one talked. It was obvious that they were in a critical situation and Samar Singh was taking a tremendous risk. A greying old officer in his khaki uniform and red beret hat grumbled slowly. "General, my humble suggestion is we call for a ceasefire and negotiate with Asha Rao. This is going to be a war in which nobody can win and there would be a general holocaust again. If you want, I can go with a white flag and ask them to come for talks. Impossible situations demand impossible remedies."

There was a bit of silence for a few minutes as General Samar Singh thought. Then there was a big loud bang of gun and the old officer collapsed with a bleeding wound in his chest.

"This is my reply to anybody who goes against my command" said the General in a hoarse but quivering voice. "Remove his body and obey my orders till the end and that is an order binding on you both Chiefs and all others. It's me who is in charge here. Life or death, this is final and I do not want any free advice or opinion however sincere it maybe. Now go and hide in the chamber of mirrors which guards the last cache of Missile system. And wait until she comes. And kill her after she opens the system with her device and hand print."

The two officers mumbled, "Yes General!" and disappeared. There was then nothing except the eerie silence in the underground bunker headquarters of the General, only interrupted by the beeps of the monitors or the humming of the air conditioners.

Chapter 22

Crypt of Death

The Sun was setting over the city, casting a red glow over the ruins and rubble. Asha Rao looked out of the window of the helicopter, clutching her gun and her VR glasses. She felt a mix of fear and determination, knowing that this was the final mission to end General Samar Singh's tyranny and save the world from a nuclear disaster. She turned to her boyfriend, Sathya who was piloting the helicopter. He gave her a reassuring smile and a thumbs up. He had been with her since the beginning, when they escaped from the forest guest house and joined the Phoenix resistance group. He was brave, loyal, and skilled, and she loved him more than anything. Next to her was Dheeraj, the computer specialist who became a close associate since the days of wandering in the wasteland after the nuclear catastrophe. He was wearing a headset and a laptop, ready to hack into the General's underground headquarters. He was a genius with codes and algorithms, and he had helped them bypass many security systems and traps along the way. He was also a good friend, always cracking jokes and making them laugh. Behind her was Dr.Ram, the middle-aged doctor. He was holding a medical kit and a tranquilizer gun, prepared to treat any injuries or casualties. He was a former colleague of the General, and he knew the secrets of his underground bunker. He had defected to the Phoenix group after witnessing the General's atrocities and experiments. He was a wise and compassionate man, and he had taught them a lot about the history and the science of the Last City. And then there was Indrani, the AI in woman's hologram shape. She was projected often from a device implanted in Asha's brain and she was their guide and ally. She was the one who contacted them and revealed the General's plan to launch the last weapons, a series of nuclear missiles that would wipe out the remaining life on the planet. She was the one who gave them the coordinates and the codes to access the bunker. She was the one who helped them evade the General's drones and soldiers. She was more than a machine; she was a friend. They were the last hope for humanity, and they knew it. They reached the outskirts of the bunker, where the first defence system was located. It was a massive metal gate, guarded by two turrets and a dozen soldiers. Sathya flew the helicopter low and fast, dodging the bullets and rockets. Asha and Dheeraj opened fire from the windows, taking out the soldiers and the turrets. Dr. Ram injected himself with a tranquilizer, hoping to survive the impact. Indrani hacked into the gate's control panel and opened it just in time. The helicopter crashed through the gate and landed in a heap of metal and fire. They quickly got out of the wreckage and ran towards the second defence system. It was a maze of tunnels and corridors, filled with traps and sensors. Indrani guided them through the VR glasses, showing them the maps and the locations. They avoided the lasers, the mines, and the cameras, and reached the third defence system. It was a huge steel door, locked by a complex code and a fingerprint scanner. Dheeraj plugged his laptop into the door's interface and started to crack the code. Indrani scanned the General's fingerprint from a database and sent it to Dheeraj's laptop. The door opened, and they entered the bunker. They were greeted by a scene of horror and madness. The bunker was a massive underground complex, filled with weapons, machines, and experiments. They saw rows of missiles, ready to launch. They saw tanks of chemicals, glowing and bubbling. They saw cages of mutants, screaming and writhing. They saw monitors of the General, laughing and taunting. They saw Viplav and his colleagues, dead and mutilated. He was the leader of the Phoenix group, and he had led the first wave of the attack. He and his team had sacrificed themselves to distract the General and his forces, and to create an opening for Asha and her team. They had fought bravely and valiantly, but they had fallen one by one. Asha felt a surge of grief and anger and swore to avenge them. She and her team split up, and headed to their respective targets. Sathya went to the missile control room, and tried to disable the launch sequence. Dr Ram went to the chemical lab, and tried to neutralize the toxins. Dheeraj went to the computer core and tried to shut down the power. Asha went to the

General's office, and tried to confront him. She kicked the door open, and pointed her gun at the General. He was sitting on a leather chair, behind a wooden desk. He was wearing a military uniform, decorated with medals and badges. He was an old man, with a bald head and a white beard. He had a scar on his left eye, and a smirk on his lips. He looked at Asha, and clapped his hands. "Bravo, bravo, my dear. You have done well."

Asha did not say anything or greet him. Here was the man who was responsible for all the misery of the world and still contemplating to do more.

She lifted the gun and pointed at him.

"General Uncle. "Your time is over. You have done unspeakable harm to the country. Now tell me how to disable the nuclear weapons remaining with you."

The General grunted. "It is your father who did this. He activated the sequence by AI".

"But you were responsible because you starred a revolt and were marching against him. You were his friend but cheated him. He activated only a simulation but somewhere it faltered. Now don't waste time. Tell or I will cripple and kill you slowly."

A few soldiers came and stood in the doorway, but Samar Singh raised a hand stopping them.

"I will not tell any details."

Asha shot him in the leg with a loud thud.

There was a screeching cry of pain from his mouth. "Next I will hit your testicles. And blow your eyes. You will suffer horribly but do not die. If you tell I will leave you for medical aid. Or kill you painlessly depending on my mood." Asha shouted with so much fury that even the soldiers were shocked and stopped in their tracks.

"No, no …I will tell. Go to the hall of mirrors! There is a blue barrel. There is a slot for the device given by your father and it will ask for the handprint of yours and password. You know the password I think. That's all. It will activate them, but you must push the button of self-destruct sequence. Then you run. It will cause an implosion here in 15 minutes. You will die if you stay. Now save me please. Don't kill me! Please have pity!" The dictator entreated.

There were a flurry of shots and she fired him in the heart till he became motion less. Indrani shouted in her mechanical voice. "Run to the mirror room!"

The soldiers with guns advanced and started firing. Asha Rao dodged the bullets and crouched. Then at that very time there was a big bang of explosives, blinding light and thick smoke. The soldiers were shocked and stopped in their tracks. It was a simulation caused by Indrani. Asha put her VR glasses and ran.

Asha Rao crouched in the shadows, her gloved fingers tracing the contours of the ancient blueprint. The underground bunker lay before her, a crypt of death, guarded by General Samar Singh's loyalists. The cache held the last remaining nuclear warheads, a grim testament to humanity's folly. The air tasted of decay and desperation. Asha's heart drummed in sync with the Geiger counter strapped to her wrist. She had infiltrated the dictator's stronghold, her resolve unyielding. The fate of the fractured world rested on her shoulders. She could enter The Mirrored Chamber by negotiating through the labyrinth of pathways with VR glasses and aided by AI Indrani's maps. She tiptoed through the serpentine corridors, her footsteps muffled by dust. The mirrored chamber awaited. It was the heart of the bunker. Twenty adjustable mirrors adorned the walls, their surfaces tarnished by time. Each mirror held a secret: a reflection pattern that betrayed any movement within the room. She adjusted the mirrors subtly, redirecting radio waves emitted by hidden antennae. The system, devised by renegade scientists, could detect even the slightest shift, a millimetres' tremor. There was the Blue Barrel in the centre. And it had a central slot by the side of which a handprint was shining in red glow. At the centre stood the blue barrel, an innocuous container concealing death. It was General Samar Singh's prized possession. Asha had learned of its existence from coded messages etched into the margins of forbidden poetry sent into her brain by Indrani. She whispered her father's name, drawing strength from memories of Vikram Rao, the man who had once led the nation. His voice echoed in her mind:

"Redemption lies in sacrifice." She put her hand on the palm shaped slot. It became green recognising her. A panel glowed and asked in a female voice. "Welcome. Now type your password to start the sequence of activation or deactivation. Be abundantly careful. This could be dangerous."

"The Countdown started now." thought Asha. Her pulse quickened. She had minutes, perhaps seconds. The world outside hungered for salvation. The Phoenix Collective, a clandestine network now destroyed and barely in existence awaited her signal. She typed the password *Rakshana 2044*. Immediately lights came on in the barrel and sounds of wheels stirring were audible. Still there was something more to do as Indrani the AI programmed her almost talking in her brain. She unsheathed the plasma cutter, its blade humming with defiance. The blue barrel yielded, revealing the dormant warheads. Asha's breath hitched. It was the last line of defence. Sparks danced as she severed wires, dismantling the triggers. The warheads would never detonate. Asha's tears blurred her vision. She whispered apologies to the ghosts of those lost, the cities turned to ash. The Geiger counter fell silent. The mirrored room held its breath. The lights were extinguished. And a voice said "Deactivating in 15 minutes. Implosion warning. Vacate the place and go to 3 kilometres at least. This is real and not a drill."

Asha ran through the corridors with the maps in her glasses showing the way and the red dot flicker showing the exit of the bunker. She had no clue where others were but the same warning sounded throughout the bunker with alarm beeping like the howling of a wolf. And as she exited she looked back at General Samar Singh's lifeless body lying in his room and the dead body guards on the floor.

"It was over. Now run for life she said to herself." Indrani now in her brain came out behind and appeared in front as the female hologram and said. "Success! Deactivation complete. Now run to the direction of coordinates I am showing. The getaway helicopter is waiting."

"Another one?"

"Yes! We had hijacked it and kept it. Sathya was on the job. No problem. Hope others will join."

They soon were at the open place where helicopter was waiting, and rotors were turning already.

They all came back, Sathya, Dheeraj and lastly Dr Ram limping from the shadows. Asha ignited the flare, the blue flames illuminating the darkness. The Phoenix Collective would see. The people of Delhi would know. As the bunker crumbled, Asha emerged as a phoenix rising from the ashes. The exiled Prime Minister's daughter had rewritten destiny. The warheads were no more. And so, in the ruins of General Samar Singh's tyranny, hope flickered, a fragile flame in the last city.

Chapter 23

Civil War

Even though it was an implosion there was considerable havoc around the main bunker of General Samar Singh. There was a huge fire with black smoke emanating from it, but it definitely was not the mushroom type. There surely were flames and they destroyed up to half a kilometre around the defence headquarters. Ashes were flying around and the citizens of Delhi. The rich who were living in protected bunkers and the poor who were living in shelters in the slums, all were in a panic and started marching towards the headquarters of the erstwhile dictator to see the cause of explosions and destruction.

They huddled in a nearby building about ten kilometres from the place of the fire, Asha Rao Dheeraj the computer specialist, Sathya the pilot and Dr Ram who was always anxious to treat the injured but prevented entry into the place of the conflagration by his colleagues. Asha Rao said "What should we do now? Should we address the people? Should we start a new Government? But how?"

"Is it not your responsibility?" asked Sathya.

"But where are the resources and how can you lead a city completely destroyed and frequently threatened by radiation sickness, acid rain and shortage of food supplies and with unhealthy water?" Asked Dheeraj.

"You should have had a plan before destroying General Samar Singh. But I am only concerned about treating the injured and give them some hygienic food. The destroyed city was being supported by the dictator with whatever meagre supplies he had even though it was a very unequal and cruel system. The phoenix collective may help. But the leader Viplav is now dead. Soon there will be food riots, gangs of hooligans attacking the rich in their bunkers to steal their food and money. Do we have any mechanism to control all this? We should meet the cabinet of General Samar Singh who could control the police and the military. We can't fight any of these robbers, hooligans and marauders on our own."

"So what should we do?" pondered Asha Rao. "Indrani! Can you give us some feedback on what is happening in the city after the implosion and destruction of the lost nuclear bombs?"

Indrani the human female shaped hologram now appeared in front of Asha Rao. She was just like any human female wearing blue jeans and t-shirt and her golden hair and blue eyes twinkled with flickering light as she spoke. "I found that there are a few networks still operating in the world and I can access some of the footage of drone cameras which were previously employed by the defence ministry of the Government of General Samar Singh. I can see groups of people crowding around the main area of the Defence headquarters which is in flames. It is my advice to you not to interfere in the present turmoil. There are obviously two groups among the people of Delhi now namely those who are supporting phoenix collective which was led by Viplav (now we do not know who) and the other group being the supporters of Samar Singh who are rich and still powerful with their money and food supplies."

"I wish we could have something to eat." Sathya said. "It is futile to sit here and speculate. I am just starving!"

"Can you visualise a nearby supermarket or a mall where there is some food available? "Asked Asha Rao addressing the AI.

Indrani conjured up a map of nearby areas which formed in front of her eyes like a transparent hologram. They were in a street adjacent to the previous Safdarjung market. And slowly a big mall with a board written on it "*Needs Mall*" appeared. It seemed desolate and unoccupied. Let's go there and search for some processed food or bread and things like that. With luck we can find them." said Sathya.

"You are always hungry," laughed Asha Rao. Dheeraj said "Why not, we all deserve some nourishing food before we decide the next course of action. Indrani can you lead us to the Needs mall? Just scout for any dangerous elements there!" Indrani said "It seems to be a lonely spot, so far. You can make it on foot within 10 minutes. There could be some food available but of course I too am running out of charge. You have to charge me there. You can take rest there and we can discuss the options. Now please walk outside one by one. Check for any soldiers or hooligans and proceed slowly towards the mall."

All of them slowed down, tiptoed outside the house where they hid until then and slowly proceeded towards the mall which was there blocks away on a curved lonely street.

As soon as they reached the mall they ran inside and searched all the floors one by one and succeeded in finding at one place some packets of bread, some canned milk and nuts. There were some tomatoes and oranges in the fruit store also. All of them quickly grabbed the food and started eating. Indrani just stood at plug point and her glow disappeared except for a twinkling red spot on her forehead indicating that she was charging herself.

"It is a tremendous intelligent machine but still its weak point is in its dependency on battery power. It has to charge itself every 48 hours. What is the use of these inventions? "said Dr.Ram. "Moreover it is an implant in your brain and would give you headaches and seizures or hallucinations. It collides with your own memory and judgement. Why did your father make such a device?" Asha said, "Obviously he intended secrecy and security and he wanted only me to have access to it. As you can see, it did help us so far. It can be hidden as well as visible. But yes I am suffering from headache and images of known and unknown persons and memories of childhood and ne and had a nosebleed the other day. I guess I must get rid of it as soon as our purpose is over. Or I will go mad." They barely finished eating their food and were getting some strength in their tired limbs as the power went off in the Mall. They heard noises outside and running footsteps and gunshots in the street.

Indrani came to power instantly and a glow entered the brain of Asha Rao again. Now Asha Rao could see what Indrani could see and she said "Hide all of you behind some cupboards or racks. There are a dozen people outside in masks and with guns. They have started looting already." The four of them hid themselves on the fourth floor behind a large almirah storing some gunny bags with obviously some waste material. Asha said "I hope that the looters may not come searching for waste material here."

Soon the whole mall was crowded with people grabbing whatever they could have access to and fighting among themselves in the local language of Hindi and possibly killing one or more amongst them fighting for the food. All this went on for half an hour and then they all disappeared outside.

There was silence for fifteen minutes and Asha could see before her eyes that the group of hooligans with their guns were running away outside. "I think we are safe now. We can come out and we have to seriously think of our options." She said as she came out of the hiding. There are only two options for us now. One is to lead the resistance forces of the poor and in need of food and shelter and help treatment for their sickness and the other option is to search for my father Vikram Rao who has fled away and possibly hiding in the South. It is obvious that we cannot lead the people without much weapons. The AI Indrani is with us, but we have no access to guns or anything. Soon there will be a civil war in Delhi and people will destroy each other. I can say that we have to go to the South on our helicopter and find out where Vikram Rao is hiding and ask him to lead the people again and start reconstruction of the Government and country." As Asha was talking like this there were sounds of huge explosions and gun fights in the city. There were a few planes flying in the sky and were dropping bombs on the city. It was very evident that there was a civil war going on and this civil war would be between the forces who were remaining still loyal to the dead General Samar Singh and the ordinary citizens, slum dwellers and the resistance forces who were running on the roads. The civil war for food and survival started and was going on. It will go on.

Chapter 24

To the South

It was a difficult time. Asha Rao had to decide the course of action on which side to be on. It's one thing to fight along with the resistance forces when Viplav and his organization were there and it is another thing to go to them now when they are a disorganised group and are fighting against the military even though the General is dead. Indrani, can you contact my father Vikram Rao and take advice? He should have made some communication code to contact you. After all he was the person who had made the device and asked to implant you in my brain. He must have had some clues to lead us to his hiding place."

Indrani said in her metallic voice as her eyes twinkled and there was a bluish glow around her head. "Asha I am trying to get the signals from him. But I am not able to get any message. But I can trace out the path he has taken by retrieving the old records in my memory. They point to a direction from where his plane had started to the place where he had landed. It is probably in the South of

India towards Hyderabad or any other surrounding city. More than this I cannot estimate his exact location."

"Can you give him a message telling him about our location and that we have eliminated General Samar Singh?"

"That is what exactly I am doing Asha. There are only a few Internet networks now existing in India as many cables and satellites have been destroyed nearby. But some hackers, some networks still operate and International Space Station is still orbiting around the Earth. It has escaped the nuclear Holocaust. There is a team of multiracial and multinational crew on the ISS. There are some networks which operate secretly to communicate with each other. They could either be the military or the resistance forces or others who are freelancers. I will try to access the movements of the Chief Minister in Hyderabad, Chennai and other southern cities from their movements and communications. We may come to one conclusion where Vikram Rao is in that city by their movement coordinates. There is a remote chance of succeeding but still I would try. It will take a day or two." "Fair enough," said Asha. Sathya said "We will wait until Indrani gives us some course of action. Now let us take some rest. And see how to get food and how to hide when a war is raging on. Dheeraj and you go out after the dusk to find out any place or hotel which is abandoned, and we will hide there. Before this evening, we will try to make some food and rations for about two days. Then we can start. I hope we still have our helicopter near the Defence headquarters. Trying to fly in the helicopter to the South is first option."

It was about noon and there was a lull in the firing as evidenced by the silence in the city. Obviously both sides were resting for lunch.

"Sathya and Dheeraj, you go out and see whether you can get some food for two days. It could be frozen food or canned food and especially bottled water whichever is available in the abandoned stores. If not, we will find tap water, but river water and lakes are contaminated with radiation." Asha said. "We will wait here. Be careful."

Sathya and Dheeraj went out and Doctor Ram rested at a corner place in the mall and tried to go for a short nap. Said Asha to Indrani the hologram. "Enter my brain again and I will visualise all the information that you are having. Is it possible?"

"I am programmed to execute any order you give me. You are my administrator. I must follow your commands. I will enter your brain. Sooner than later I have to leave your brain as it would damage your neurological status. Please remember that as I stay in your brain I will utilise the energy from your body and work. When I stay outside I have to take the energy from outside sources" said Indrani the AI and there in a flash the hologram disappeared and her glow entered the brain of Asha through the small device implanted in the occipital lobe in the back of her head. But for a few hours Asha had viewed hallucinations in front of her. It was as if she was travelling in an unknown land. She could see mountains, she could see rivers, she could see forests like she could see them from a plane. And she could see one red dot. The red dot was mentioning Vikram and as she followed the dot. The dot went down somewhere in latitude in the South of India disappeared.

She had a severe headache and a reeling sensation and something wet was coming from her nose. When she touched it it was blood. The implant was taking most of her energy and causing her brain a tumultuous effect. Soon she became unconscious and still.

She woke up only when Dr Ram was calling her repeatedly and slapping her face to wake her up.

She slowly opened her eyes as the Doctor came into focus.

"You were seizing." he said. "I gave you diazepam injection as better medicine is not with me. Listen to me Asha. You throw out that device of AI from your head!

"Let us work on our own. It is dangerous for your health, and you could get insane or even die. What were you doing?"

"I could calculate the place of hiding of my father Vikram Rao. He is in Hyderabad Deccan, and he has travelled and not moved from there. We will have to travel there."

"OK! But you remove that thing and give a program to her to stay outside your brain. You could die using it."

"Ok." Asha Rao said weakly.

"Now come out, Indrani and charge yourself Dr.Ram said. Now I will remove that disc from your brain."

Sathya and Dheeraj just entered and Sathya ran to her. "What happened?"

As they were told the event that happened Sathya said. "Let us remove it and we will go on our own. Enough is enough. AI seems to be dangerous."

"But we need it for navigation."

"Use it as a computer from outside, not as an implant."

Without further discussion Sathya and Ram turned Asha on her back and removed the disc circular from her head.

The glow has come out and manifested as Indrani.

"I have charged only for 12 hours."

"Deactivate. We will use you when we reach our destination."

Asha sat up holding her head.

The headache and images are gone. What a relief!

"Brain computer interface is still an evolving technology. Your dad used it to save you in an emergency."

"Let us travel to the Southern City of Hyderabad on our own and meet him."

The AI Indrani slowly faded and disappeared into the circular disc held in the hand of Dheeraj.

Chapter 25

Harbhajan 2

Harbhajan was in a dazed state. He was wandering among the grotesquely spread out corpses on the road outside the bunker of Defence Headquarters. A flutter of images floated in front of his eyes. His wife, kids and his old father looking sadly at him. Memories of the child crying with hunger, the military trucks taking him to work, his joining the resistance and partaking in the sabotage operations. Then suddenly it all came back to him. He was with Dheeraj and Sathya and Asha Rao the erstwhile PM'S daughter and all of them went into the bunker. What happened there? There was only a memory of an explosion in front of his eyes and then even without VR glasses or any artificial implant in his brain Harbhajan Singh was slowly remembering everything. They did destroy General Samar Singh. That was a splendid achievement. What happened to his family? Where were they? He looked around and there was nothing except black smoke as far as he could see. There was no doubt that it was the effect of the nuclear implosion which happened in the bunker. There must have been panic and havoc in the city. People must have been migrating out of fear of another explosion but it was unlikely that anybody would have been killed by just what they did. It was a self-destructing implosion and could have damaged the area around a kilometre only. Where were the others?

He waded through the bodies and the rubble trying to find out any help and for the signs of his companions. There was terrible pain in in his left leg and he could tolerate it only with enormous self control and pressure. It was obvious that there was a fracture in the leg. Where could he find medical help? And as he searched around and dragged himself with enormous pain he could hear the sound of footsteps and people talking. First it came as a gurgling faintly and then as a hoarse cry from his throat. And then it became a loud wail of a wounded person. And then he fainted again because of loss of blood and severe pain. It was many hours after that the rescue health workers of the resistance forces found him unconscious and carried him on makeshift stretchers to a tent where they were attending to the wounded and the sick. As he opened his eyes after a few days a health volunteer recognised him and asked him "Are you not Harbhajan Singh who lived the *ChandniChowk mohalla*? I know your family. I was living in the same area."

Harbhajan Singh became alert and asked "How are they, please take me to them. Are they well, are they having food and proper facilities? Please take me to them." Harbhajan's leg was plastered in a splint and his wounds were attended and he recovered now. And the volunteer said, do not worry Harbhajan, your family is in the refugee camp organised by the phoenix collective. We are all liberated from General Samar Singh's dictatorial rule but we have to fend for ourselves. There is no more Government. We have to find food, water and a clean environment for our families." There was an ancient ambulance van outside with a big Red Cross mark on it. Harbhajan Singh soon was taken to the refugee camp organised by the phoenix collective. And as he was being transported he asked the attendant in the van "Do you have any idea where the PM'S daughter is? I was with them when we attacked the bunker. I helped them. What happened to them at all?"

"No Idea, My friend! These are bad times. There is a lot of confusion and anarchy and those people who went to search for the PM's daughter and her group could not find them at all. Is it not a disgrace to think that even the PM'S daughter had not stayed back to help us in a disaster? In any case there is nothing to help us too. Most of the useful things and productive things in the capital are destroyed. This is a post nuclear scenario where there is no means of getting food, or proper water except through the resources we are getting from looting and paid and brought from across the border of other countries. In this anarchic situation we have to hope for the best and fight till the last. Thank your stars that you are going to meet your family who are just waiting for you every minute" As the ambulance stopped before a huge tent with a big red plus mark on its doors Harbhajan was transported inside.

And it was the best moment of his life to find his wife and kids waiting for him crying and smiling alternatively.

When all that was over he asked "Where is Papa, only to learn that his old father had died long ago. Soon Harbhajan mingled himself with others in the tent serving the other wounded and sick people. But as days and months passed with half meals, dark clouds and frequent acid rains and constant struggle for resources, the thought never left in the back of his mind that the group of the PM'S daughter Asha Rao had forgotten him and left for some unknown destination without him.

Chapter 26

The Journey

They were sitting in the helicopter sailing through the black smoky clouds at about a thousand kilometres distance from Delhi. Asha Rao, Dheeraj and Dr Ram were sitting in the cabin while Sathya the pilot was driving the helicopter. In the aftermath of the nuclear implosion around the bunker there was no way to go back to the people in Delhi and lead them to any meaningful rehabilitation without any resources in their hands. They discussed pros and cons of staying and going to the South searching for their PM whom they located with the help of the artificial intelligence Indrani. With luck they could find him in the city of Hyderabad. The city was about two thousand kilometres from Delhi. After wandering a long time in the rubble around the bunker of General Samar Singh and spending a few nights discussing the advantages and disadvantages Sathya and Dheeraj could find a helicopter which was still in working order.

And now that the artificial intelligence device of Indrani was removed from her brain, Asha Rao had no more help of Indrani to navigate or look at the directions where to go. But the flipside was she had fewer headaches and clear mind. Dheeraj could use his hacking skills and started to fly the helicopter. It is a safe bet that they could reach Hyderabad in a day. The only question was fuel. Can a helicopter travel the distance of 2000 kilometres and how much fuel was required?

The answer to this question depended on the type and model of the helicopter, as well as the speed, altitude, and weather conditions. The average fuel consumption of a helicopter ranged from 6 to 16 gallons per hour for a small piston-powered helicopter, and from 20 to several hundreds of gallons per hour for a larger turbine-powered helicopter. The range of a typical helicopter could vary from 300 to 800 kilometers (186 to 497 miles) before requiring refuelling. Therefore, to travel the distance of about 2000 kilometers (932 miles) from Delhi to Hyderabad, a helicopter would need to refuel at least once or twice, depending on the model and the fuel capacity. For example, a Bell 47 helicopter, which has a fuel consumption of 15 gallons per hour and a range of 370 kilometers (230 miles), would need to refuel three times and use about 60 gallons of fuel. A Sikorsky UH-60 Black Hawk helicopter, which has a fuel consumption of 137 gallons per hour and a range of 592 kilometres (368 miles), would need to refuel twice and use about 410 gallons of fuel.

It was a Bell 47 helicopter they have managed to steal again and start flying towards South with Sathya the pilot taking control.

Asha Rao looked out of the window of the helicopter and felt a surge of mixed emotions. She had just witnessed the destruction of General Samar Singh's last weapons in his bunker, thanks to the brave sacrifice of her father, the former Prime Minister of India, who had stayed behind. She had also learned from Indrani, the artificial intelligence in the form of a female hologram, that her father was still alive and hiding in a secret bunker somewhere in Hyderabad. She hoped that she would see him again soon, and that he would be proud of her for continuing his fight against the tyrannical regime that had plunged the country into chaos and misery. She glanced at her companions, who were also looking weary and exhausted. Sathya, her childhood friend and the pilot of the helicopter, was focused on the controls, trying to avoid the acid rain and the dark clouds that filled the sky. Dheeraj, the computer specialist who had hacked into Indrani's system and retrieved the vital information, was checking his laptop for any signs of enemy activity. Dr. Ram, the middle-aged doctor who had treated their wounds and illnesses, was resting his eyes, clutching a first-aid kit. They had been flying for almost four hours, covering more than half of the distance from Delhi to Hyderabad. They had refuelled once at a deserted airfield, where they had encountered some scavengers who had tried to rob them. They had managed to escape, but not without some damage to the helicopter and some injuries to themselves. They had no idea if they were being followed or tracked by the dictator's remaining army, which had deployed drones and missiles to hunt down any rebels or dissidents. Asha checked her watch and saw that it was almost noon. She wondered how long it would take them to reach Hyderabad, and if they would find her father there. She also wondered what kind of world they would live in after the nuclear catastrophe that had devastated the planet. She had seen the horrors of radiation sickness, famine, disease, and violence that had claimed millions of lives. She had also seen the resilience and courage of the people who had resisted the oppression and fought for freedom and justice. She hoped that there was still a chance for peace and recovery, and that she could play a role in it. She was about to say something to her friends, when she heard a loud beep from Dheeraj's laptop. She turned to him and saw his face turn pale.

"What is it?" she asked.

"We have a problem," he said. "There's a drone on our tail. And it's armed with a missile."

Asha felt a jolt of fear and adrenaline. She looked at Sathya, who had also heard the warning.

"Can you lose it?" she asked.

"I'll try," he said. "But it's fast and agile. And we're low on fuel and ammo."

He swerved the helicopter to the left, then to the right, trying to dodge the drone. But the drone was relentless, matching every move and closing the gap.

"Can you jam its signal?" Asha asked Dheeraj.

"I'm working on it," he said. "But it's encrypted and protected. It's not easy."

He typed furiously on his keyboard, hoping to find a way to hack into the drone's system and disable it.

"Can you shoot it down?" Asha asked Dr. Ram, who had a rifle with him.

"I'll try," he said. "But it's small and fast. And we're moving too."

He opened the window and aimed his rifle at the drone, which was now only a few hundred meters behind them. He fired a few shots, but missed.

"Damn it," he cursed.

The drone fired a missile, which streaked towards the helicopter. "Brace yourselves!" Sathya shouted.

He pulled the helicopter up, hoping to evade the missile. But it was too late. The missile hit the tail of the helicopter, causing a massive explosion. The helicopter spun out of control, losing altitude and speed. Asha felt a surge of pain and heat, as flames engulfed the cabin. She screamed, as did her friends. She saw the ground rushing towards them, and then everything went blank.

Chapter 27

Rescued

The sky was dark and the air was humid. There she was playing as a child in the garden of their home in Delhi. There was her young father Vikram Rao fondling her and playing cricket in the open yard. Then there were scenes of his political campaigns and the attack on his motorcade by the opponents of his policies. The collapsing figure of her mother in the open topped jeep in slow motion with a crimson spot of death spreading on her chest. The grief of her loss and the years of growing up with only a female servant to look after her and the evolution of her father over the years as a liberal political leader and slowly ascending up to become the PM. The happy memories of his oath taking on the Red Fort before the multitudes of joyous shouting crowds. It was vague and also was vivid. Then Sathya, her boyfriend and the pleasant evenings at the club and weekends in the White horse pub. Then there was a loud thundering sound and a mushroom cloud in the horizon. She with her friends as unseen shapes was running in the darkest night in the black showers of acid rain. They were the unknown fears of REM sleep and a flurry of nightmares. She then had become awake and was relieved. They were only dreams.

Asha opened her eyes and felt a sharp pain in her head. She smelled smoke and blood. She looked around and saw the wreckage of the helicopter, scattered across a barren field. She saw Sathya lying next to her, unconscious and bleeding from a wound on his leg. She saw Dheeraj and Dr. Ram a few meters away, also unconscious and injured. She saw the drone, smashed and burned, a few yards away. She saw the sky, dark and cloudy, with a faint glow of the sun. She tried to move, but felt a surge of pain in her chest. She realized that she had broken ribs and possibly internal injuries. She coughed and tasted blood in her mouth. She felt dizzy and weak. She wondered if they were going to die there, alone and forgotten. She heard a faint sound of voices and footsteps. She saw a group of people approaching them, carrying sticks and guns. They looked like villagers, dressed in simple clothes and turbans. They looked curious and cautious, but not hostile. They spoke in a language that Asha did not understand, but she guessed that it was Telugu, the local dialect.

One of the villagers, an old man with a white beard, came closer to Asha and examined her. He touched her pulse and looked into her eyes. He said something to the others, and they nodded. He gestured to two young men, who lifted Asha carefully and carried her to a nearby cart. They did the same for Sathya, Dheeraj, and Dr. Ram.

They loaded the cart with some of their belongings, such as the laptop, the rifle, and the first-aid kit. They left behind the rest of the helicopter and the drone, too heavy and useless to carry.

The old man climbed onto the cart and whipped the horse. The cart started to move, followed by the rest of the villagers. Asha felt the cart bumping and shaking, as it rolled along the dirt road. She felt the pain in her body, but also a faint hope in her heart. She hoped that the villagers were friendly and helpful, and not spies or traitors. She hoped that her friends would survive and recover. She hoped that they would reach Hyderabad and find her father. She hoped that they would live to see a better day. She closed her eyes and drifted into light sleep this time sensing good people have come to help.

And they really did help.

Asha and her friends were taken to a small village, where they were treated with kindness and generosity by the villagers. The old man who had rescued them was the head of the village, and he offered them his house to stay. He also arranged for a local healer to tend to their wounds and injuries. He told them that his name was Ramesh, and that he and his people were part of a resistance movement against the dictator. He said that they had heard of Asha's father, the former Prime Minister, and that they admired his courage and leadership. He said that they were willing to help them in any way they could. Asha thanked Ramesh and his people for their hospitality and support.

She told them that they were on a mission to find her father, who was hiding in a bunker in Hyderabad. She said that they had vital information that could help end the war and restore democracy. She said that they needed to reach Hyderabad as soon as possible, before the dictator's army found them. Ramesh said that he understood their urgency, but that they also needed to rest and recover. He said that the journey to Hyderabad was not easy, especially in the post-nuclear state of the world. He said that the roads were dangerous and unpredictable, with acid rain, radiation, and mutants. He said that they also had to avoid the checkpoints and patrols of the dictator's army, which had drones and missiles. He said that they would need a reliable and discreet transport, and that he would try to arrange one for them. Asha agreed to stay in the village for a few days, until they were ready to resume their travel. She and her friends spent their time resting, healing, and bonding with the villagers. They learned more about their culture, language, and history. They also shared their stories, skills, and knowledge. They ate simple but nutritious food, mostly grains, vegetables, and fruits. They drank clean water from a well. They slept on comfortable beds, under warm blankets. They felt safe and welcome, as if they had found a new family.

After four days, Ramesh told them that he had found a transport for them. He said that it was an old truck, driven by a smuggler who was part of the resistance. He said that the truck was loaded with stolen groceries and food, which he would deliver to other rebel groups along the way. He said that the truck would take them as close to Hyderabad as possible, but that they would have to walk the last 25 kilometers by themselves. He said that the truck would leave at dawn, and that they should be ready. Asha and her friends thanked Ramesh and his people for their help and hospitality. They packed their belongings, including the laptop, the rifle, and the first-aid kit. They also took some food and water, and some clothes and blankets. They hugged and said goodbye to their hosts, promising to keep in touch and to return someday. They boarded the truck, which was driven by a young man named Raju. He greeted them and told them to sit in the back, among the crates and sacks. He started the engine and drove away.

The truck was old and noisy, but it ran smoothly and steadily. Raju was a skilled and experienced driver, who knew the roads and the routes well. He avoided the main highways and the towns, and took the back roads and the fields. He also avoided the acid rain and the radiation, and took shelter under bridges and trees. He also avoided the checkpoints and the patrols, and used his contacts and his bribes to pass through. He also avoided the robbers and the mutants, and used his speed and his weapons to fight them off. Asha and her friends sat in the back of the truck, holding on to each other and to their belongings. They felt the truck bumping and shaking, as it rolled along the rough terrain. They felt the wind and the dust, as it blew through the cracks and the holes. They felt the heat and the cold, as it changed with the day and the night. They also felt the fear and the hope, as they got closer and closer to their destination. They travelled for three days and three nights, stopping only for refueling and resting. They saw the landscape change, from flat and dry, to hilly and green, to rocky and barren. They saw the cities and the villages, mostly deserted and destroyed, with only a few survivors and scavengers. They saw the signs of the nuclear catastrophe, the craters, the ruins, the skeletons, the mutants. They also saw the signs of the resistance, the graffiti, the flags, the messages, the rebels.

On the fourth day, they reached the outskirts of Hyderabad. Raju told them that he could not take them any further, as the city was under the dictator's control, and that it was too risky and too crowded. He said that they would have to walk the rest of the way, and that he would give them a map and some directions. He said that he wished them good luck and Godspeed, and that he hoped that they would find what they were looking for. He said that he would wait for them at a safe spot, and that he would take them back if they returned. Asha and her friends thanked Raju for his help and service. They got off the truck and took their belongings. They looked at the map, and saw that they had to walk south, towards the center of the city. They saw that the city was divided into zones, with different levels of security and surveillance. They saw that they had to cross several checkpoints and barriers, and that they had to avoid the drones and the missiles. They also saw that they had to find the bunker, where Asha's father was hiding, and that they had to contact him somehow.

They started to walk, following the map and the directions. They walked through the streets and the alleys, among the buildings and the vehicles. They saw the scene of Hyderabad, in the post-nuclear destroyed state, with only a few strong structures intact. They saw the Charminar, the iconic monument of the city, half-collapsed and charred. They saw the Golconda Fort, the ancient fortress of the city, reduced to rubble and ashes. They saw the Hussain Sagar Lake, the scenic lake of the city, dried up and polluted. They saw the Ramoji Film City, the largest film studio of the world, abandoned and looted.

They also saw the people of Hyderabad, the survivors and the victims, the rebels, and the loyalists, the rich and the poor. They saw the people who had fled the city, seeking refuge and safety elsewhere. They saw the people who had stayed in the city, fighting for their rights and their lives. They saw the people who had joined the resistance, risking their lives and their freedom. They saw the people who had joined the dictator, enjoying their privileges and their power.

They walked for about five hours, covering about 20 kilometers. They encountered some difficulties and dangers, such as checkpoints, patrols, drones, missiles, robbers, and mutants. They managed to overcome them, using their skills, their weapons, their contacts, and their luck. They also encountered some friends and allies, such as rebels, smugglers, hackers, and healers. They received some help and support, such as food, water, medicine, information, and guidance.

They reached the last 5 kilometres of their journey, and saw the skyline of the city centre, where the bunker was located. They saw the skyscrapers and the towers, some standing and some falling, some shining and some dark. They saw the most prominent building, the Raj Bhavan, the official residence of the Governor of the state, and the headquarters of the dictator's agent. They saw the bunker, hidden under the ground, protected by layers of concrete and steel. They saw their destination, and their hope.

They walked faster, eager to reach the bunker and to find Asha's father. They walked past the last checkpoint, using a fake ID and a bribe. Bribes were more powerful as currency was scarce. They walked past the last barrier, using a secret code and a password. They walked past the last drone, using a jammer and a decoy. They walked past the last missile, using a shield and a dodge.

They reached the entrance of the bunker, a metal door with a keypad and a scanner. They entered the code and the scan, using the information that Indrani had given them. They heard a beep and a click, and the door opened. They entered the bunker, and the door closed behind them.

They walked down a long corridor, lit by dim lights. They walked past several rooms, labelled with numbers and names. They walked past the control room, the generator room, the storage room, the medical room, the security room, the communication room. They walked past the last room, labelled with the name of Asha's father: Vikram Rao.

They opened the door, and saw a small and simple room, with a bed, a desk, a chair, a computer, a phone, and a TV. They saw a man sitting on the bed, wearing a white shirt, black pants, and a blue jacket. He had grey hair, a beard, and glasses. He looked tired and old, but also calm and wise. He looked up, and saw them.

He recognized them, and smiled. He stood up, and walked towards them. He hugged them, and welcomed them. He said that he was glad to see them, and that he was proud of them. He said that he had been waiting for them, and that he had been hoping for them.

Chapter 28

Reunion

The mixed feelings of ecstasy and sorrow were overwhelming for Asha Rao.

"Oh! My Papa…how much I missed you and how you suffered all these days!"

As all others watched silently with tearful eyes father and daughter embraced and cried for a few minutes without words. The long aftermath of the nuclear catastrophe and the stay in the bunker for many months made PM Vikram Rao pale and weak and he looked many years older and lost a lot of weight and his white moustache and beard made him look more like the benevolent patriarch he was for the whole country.

"It was our misfortune my baby, all of it was a mistake and should not have happened. Lot of our countrymen died and the whole world had plunged into destruction. And Samar Singh…?

You can forget about him. I with the help of these people destroyed him. He died in his bunker with the implosion.

This is Sathya my friend, Dheeraj and Dr.Ram. They, with the phoenix resistance forces helped us. But…

"I know…some residual forces of Samar Singh are still there. This is the Chief Minister of this state Mr.Reddy who is on my side and helped and protected me."

A tall man in white kurta and pyjama, lean face, with a curved black moustache and fierce looking eyes stepped forward.

"Greetings! Welcome Madam Asha! You and your friends are courageous. You not only survived the nuclear blast but destroyed the dictator in his den. We are on your side as Vikram Sir is a great man with democratic values and humanity and thinks of the people rather than his personal safety. Have food and take rest a while. The war is over but the final battle remains as the Governor still supports the remnants of military forces and drones of Samar Singh. But we will defeat him"

What followed was a prolonged period of rest recapitulation of all that what happened on either side, long evenings of strategy sessions and plan of a resistance war on the remaining forces of Samar Singh.

It transpired that Prime Minister Vikram Rao had pushed the button only to create an artificial scare in the revolting troops of General Samar Singh on that unfortunate day and by a quirk of fate or a mistake of the machine a real war alert had started. It started a chain reaction of nuclear attacks by artificial intelligence systems all over the world.

"I am still feeling guilty about it and repented all these months." Vikram Rao said in a week tone which sounded like that of coming from a hundred year old man. "I survived and came back to Hyderabad as Samar Singh occupied the capital anyway and started reconstructing and I had no powerful followers behind me to guide or support me to attack him."

"Do not repent father! Things happen. Mistakes do happen and perhaps anybody would have done the same in that situation. It is better not to dwell on the past but to think of what to do in the future. We have to protect the values of freedom and human rights which were being forcibly destroyed by the dead Samar Singh and his party. Because we had successfully destroyed Samar Singh and his forced and remaining nuclear missiles

A few drone force and a few more military forces have to be destroyed. That's all. God is great and we will succeed.".

Asha consoled her father constantly till he became more confident.

The Chief Minister Reddy in Hyderabad and his forces organised the planned attack on the Raj Bhavan on the he 1st of July 2045 nearly one year after the previous nuclear catastrophe. They did not have many weapons except ordinary rifles and guns and old fashioned swords and grenades. Their asset was surprise and the constant drizzling rain of the monsoon which started in July. To add to this the unpredictable acid rain which of course was gradually dwindling, and the lack of communication facilities helped the rebel troops. The Governor who stayed in a bunker under the façade of the Raj Bhavan with his advisers called for reinforcements and fighter planes but couldn't get any. A few drones appeared in the sky and dropped a bomb or two without aim or precision.

The great march of the people along with the CM and PM and Asha Rao behind was like a pageant of victory rather than the final assault.

There was firing and a few grenades thrown. There were skirmishes in the rich areas of Banjara hills Jubilee hills and Gachibowli where the rich lived in relative comfort. But soon it was all over. The very presence of PM Vikram Rao and Asha Rao and the now confirmed rumours of the death of Samar Singh made people to follow the rebel troops led by Chief Minister Reddy and Vikram Rao.

The Governor with his military advisers came out of the big iron gates of the palace with white flags and raised hands.

"I surrender to you with all my men."

There were gunshots fired but this time into the air as the celebration of victory.

"We hold no revenge. Disarm them but do not kill the Governor and his advisers. All the Governor's troops must surrender their arms and reveal the hidden bombs or drones or planes if any. The war is over. All must unite and rebuild the city and country."

PM Rao thus gave a great speech stimulating all those assembled before the palace of erstwhile Governor. There were joyous hugs and slogans praising PM Rao and CM Reddy. They all entered the palace and occupied it. We must feed the poor but there are no food supplies, or agriculture. We must tend to the sick but there are few doctors and medicines. We must bring the poor suffering people out of the crowded bunkers. We must make and build the last city. Said Rao. "Only now, the last city would be Hyderabad and not Delhi which is distant and in anarchic mode".

So the plan for Last City began. And the conferences and plans for development rebuilding the city and country went on with the help of inputs from Indrani and some other scientists who survived were recruited.

Chapter 29

Rebuilding

Even though they shifted to the Governor's palace they still had to live in the spacious underground bunkers as the Geiger counters still showed radiation at lower levels. They had to wear radiation suits when they came out for meetings. Asha and Sathya had met privately many times and decided to get married only after a complete recovery happened in the country and one never could predict the effects of radiation on offspring yet. Yet there was a determination in all of them to hatch out plans of resurrection. Dr.Ram immersed himself in the care of patients in the poor areas of old city again. Dheeraj tried to find signals and hack the communication networks damaged by the nuclear catastrophe, and was trying to communicate with the International space stations of India US and Russia which should be in the space above unaffected by the war. And he was trying to connect with perhaps some submarines which existed in the oceans. The bunker walls whispered secrets, the last remnants of governance. Asha's footsteps echoed as she approached the PM's chamber. His eyes, once fierce, now held the weight of a crumbling world.

"My dear papa and Prime Minister Vikram Rao, Asha said, "We must rise from these ashes. India needs us. "They established the Council of Hope" a group of top officers and scientists and politicians for discussions. The Chief Minister, a stoic figure, stood by the PM's side. Together, they formed the Council of Hope, eventhough it was a fragile alliance. Their mission was to reconstruct a nation fractured by war. "We have no choice," the CM said. "Our people hunger for more food than survival."

And then they made the "Blueprint of Renewal." Indrani the AI projected holographic maps, blueprints for resurrection. They would reclaim barren lands, restore infrastructure, and build anew. "Agriculture," Asha declared, "is our lifeline."

In addition they had to tame the Nuclear Winter. The sky remained veiled, a perpetual twilight. The bright Sun was a distant memory. But still science offered a glimmer of salvation.

"Hydroponics," the PM said, "and underground farms. We'll harness artificial light, grow crops in sealed chambers."

The CM nodded. "Vertical gardens, stacked like hope itself. Water Purification can be done by installing advanced water purification systems to ensure safe drinking water.

But there were challenges and considerations. One method of food production was to produce Algae which could act as a nourishing food for the starving in the absence of agriculture and products of food grains. But how to get energy to grow them. Traditional farming was not yet possible. How to produce energy? Algae cultivation required energy for lighting and temperature control. Renewable energy sources (solar, wind) could help. The growth of Algae required nutrient supply. Algae need nutrients (nitrogen, phosphorus, etc.). Synthetic nutrient solutions could replace soil. Food Diversity too was essential. While algae provided essential nutrients, a balanced diet required variety. They considered supplementing it with other foods. Post-Nuclear Winter Agriculture was a tremendous challenge. Tropical Forests, despite soot clouds, offered opportunities for limited food production. Such forests existed still in the *"Dandakaranya" and* Western *Ghats*. Warmer temperatures allowed some growth. Researchers have classified wild, edible plants into categories: fruits, leafy vegetables, seeds, nuts, roots, spices, sweets, and protein. These could sustain local inhabitants. The adaptation to nuclear winter was to develop hardy crop varieties that can withstand reduced sunlight and altered precipitation patterns.

Their vision combined resilience, innovation, and adaptability. In the darkest times.

One day Asha was awakened by a security officer "Madam, sorry to disturb you but a group of Sardars with families and children just arrived from the North and are repeatedly asking for you.

Asha rubbed her eyes and went to the gate in front. And she was too delighted to see the group of Sikhs old and young, women and children in dusty torn clothes and emaciated faces. In front of the group was Harbhajan Singh tall weather beaten and full of dust and blisters on his face but strong and courageous as always.

"We walked all the way, we beat the marauders, mutants and thieves and acid rain and nuclear winter. And we came for you." He said.

"Welcome! Harbhajan! How happy I am. And we will take care of all of you. And you will take part in the reconstruction of the country.

They were given food, clothes and medical treatment and soon would join them in the efforts of rebuilding the city and country.

Asha and the PM, guided by the multinational crew aboard the international space station, embarked also on a new daring mission. Their goal: to find a new home among the stars.

And then another day Dheeraj came running as they were having lunch in the bunker.

"I got a signal from the Indian orbiting space station and started talking to them. I explained everything and the situation."

"We can plan for finding a suitable planet to migrate to!" said Asha. "Even though it is a distant possibility."

"Let them explore the planets to inhabit. We will make plans. Said Vikram Rao. One day it may be possible!"

That would be the future! Interstellar Exploration was definitely possible. By 2055 CE, advancements in propulsion technology could allow for interstellar travel. Perhaps they would discover a distant exoplanet, a pale blue dot orbiting a distant Sun. It could be a new hope! Just like your name Asha."Said the Chief Minister Reddy. "Anything is possible. At least we will show some solutions to the next generation. It could be the New Eden for humanity. The planet, christened "New Eden," may hold promise. Its atmosphere may breathe life, its oceans may have alien wonders. But it may not happen in the near future. We have to build a spaceship and find energy to travel light years and the means to settle there with Terra farms and other equipment."

"We can at least make a beginning." Said the Prime minister.

Alternatively, Asha and the PM focused their energies on Earth's renewal too. The nuclear winter would wane surely and pockets of green would emerge. The bunkers would become sanctuaries till then and the algae farms would thrive.

Scientists started to develop solar sails, giant reflective sheets propelled by sunlight. These sails could carry humanity to Mars or beyond. But can they sustain life?

And nearby in the solar system Mars was a planet only three years away. The Red Planet too beckoned. Asha gazed at its rusty surface, wondering if it could be terraformed. The PM, older now, dreamt of a Martian garden. Asha stood at the crossroads. New Eden, Mars, or Earth's rebirth? The multinational crew debated endlessly. The world watched.

Asha transmitted a signal, a binary poem, into the cosmos. It read… *"Wherever we go, we carry Earth's legacy. We are stardust and resilience."*

Both paths held beauty and challenges. Whether Asha gazed at the distant stars or tended to Earth's fragile shoots, her journey was a testament to our shared humanity.

"The Last City" was built with a balance between Earth's reconstruction and the eternal quest for interplanetary colonization.

Asha Rao and her team's dream was both poignant and optimistic.

The End.